M000312508

# STEM Labs for Life Science
## Grades 6–8

**Authors:** Schyrlet Cameron and Carolyn Craig
**Editor:** Mary Dieterich
**Proofreaders:** April Albert and Margaret Brown

COPYRIGHT © 2017 Mark Twain Media, Inc.

ISBN 978-1-62223-640-4

Printing No. CD-404261

Mark Twain Media, Inc., Publishers
Distributed by Carson-Dellosa Publishing LLC

**Visit us at www.carsondellosa.com**

# Table of Contents

# To the Teacher

**STEM** is an acronym for **Science, Technology, Engineering,** and **Mathematics**. STEM education is an initiative designed to get students interested in these career fields. STEM learning emphasizes students gaining knowledge and developing skills needed for a twenty-first-century workforce.

STEM Labs is a three-book series. The books in the series include *STEM Labs for Life Science, STEM Labs for Physical Science,* and *STEM Labs for Earth & Space Science*. The series provides fun and meaningful integrated activities designed to cultivate student interest in topics of the STEM fields. All the activities in the series are lab investigations that support the national standards: Next Generation Science Standard (NGSS) developed by the National Teachers of Science Association (NTSA), National Council of Teachers of Mathematics Standards (NCTM), Standards for Technology Literacy (ITEA), and Common Core State Standards (CCSS). Each book includes:

- **Instructional Resources:** A set of informational handouts to guide students in successfully completing STEM investigations.
- **Lab Challenges:** Investigations promoting the STEM fields (science, technology, engineering, and mathematics). Labs emphasize designing an object, process, model, or system to solve a problem.
- **Rubrics:** Scoring guides explain the set of criteria used for assessing the projects.

*STEM Labs for Life Science* contains 26 lab activities that challenge students to apply scientific inquiry, content knowledge, and technological design to solve a real-world problem. Key components of every lab activity are creativity, teamwork, communication, and critical thinking. Each lab activity requires students to:

- **Research:** Students find out what is already known about the topic being investigated.
- **Collaborate:** Students complete activities in collaborative groups. They are encouraged to communicate openly, support each other, and respect contributions of members as they pool perspectives and experiences toward solving a problem.
- **Design:** Students use creativity and imagination to design an object, process, model, or system. Students test the design, record data, and analyze and interpret results.
- **Reflect:** Students think back on the process in a way that further promotes higher-order thinking.

*STEM Labs for Life Science* is written for classroom teachers, parents, and students. This book can be used to supplement existing curriculum or enhance after-school or summer-school programs.

# STEM Education

The STEMs of Learning: **Science**, **Technology**, **Engineering**, and **Mathematics** is an initiative designed to get students interested in these career fields. In 2009, the National Academy of Engineering (NAE) and the National Research Council (NRC) reported that there was a lack of focus on the science, technology, engineering, and mathematics (STEM) subjects in K–12 schools. This creates concerns about the competitiveness of the United States in the global market and the development of a workforce with the knowledge and skills needed to address technical and technological issues.

| STEM Education | |
|---|---|
| **STEM** | **Knowledge and Skills Needed to Address Technical and Technological Issues** |
| **Science** | **Basic science process skills** include the basic skills of classifying, observing, measuring, inferring, communicating, predicting, manipulating materials, replicating, using numbers, developing vocabulary, questioning, and using cues.<br><br>**Integrated science skills** (more complex skills) include creating models, formulating a hypothesis, generalizing, identifying and controlling variables, defining operationally, recording and interpreting data, making decisions, and experimenting. |
| **Technology** | **Design process** includes identifying and collecting information about everyday problems that can be solved by technology. It also includes generating ideas and requirements for solving the problems. |
| **Engineering** | **Design process** includes identifying a problem or design opportunity; proposing designs and possible solutions; implementing the solution; evaluating the solution and its consequences; and communicating the problem, processes, and solution. |
| **Mathematics** | **Mathematical skills** include the ability to use problem-solving skills, formulate problems, develop and apply a variety of strategies to solve problems, verify and interpret results, and generalize solutions and strategies to new problems. Students also need to be able to communicate with models, orally, in writing, and with pictures and graphs; reflect and clarify their own thinking; use the skills of reading, listening, and observing to interpret and evaluate ideas; and be able to make conjectures and convincing arguments. |

# Characteristics of a STEM Lesson

**STEM** education emphasizes a new way of teaching and learning that focuses on hands-on inquiry and open-ended exploration. It allows students with diverse interests, abilities, and experiences to develop skills they will need in the 21st-century workforce. It is a shift away from the teacher presenting information and covering science topics to the teacher guiding and assisting students in problem-solving while encouraging them to take the lead in their own learning.

## Characteristics of a STEM Lesson

- Stimulates the curiosity and interest of both girls and boys
- Emphasizes hands-on, inquiry-based learning
- Addresses both math and science standards
- Encourages the use of and/or creation of technology
- Involves the engineering design process
- Stresses collaborative teamwork

## 10 Steps in a STEM Lesson

Students are presented with a challenge to design a model, process, or system to solve a problem. They work on the challenge in collaborative teams of three or four students, depending on the STEM lesson. Each team follows a set of problem-solving steps in order to find a solution.

Step #1:     Research the problem and solutions.

Step #2:     Brainstorm ideas about how to design a model, process, or system to solve the problem.

Step #3:     Draw a diagram of the model, process, or system.

Step #4:     Construct a prototype.

Step #5:     Test the prototype.

Step #6:     Evaluate the performance of the prototype.

Step #7:     Identify how to improve the design of the prototype.

Step #8:     Make the needed changes to the prototype.

Step #9:     Retest and reevaluate the prototype.

Step #10:    Share the results.

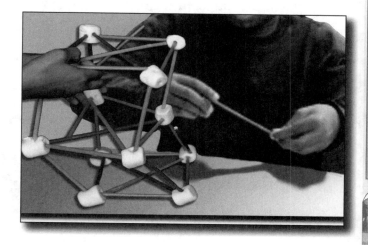

# Collaborative Learning Teams

**Collaborative learning** is a successful teaching strategy in which small groups of students, each with different levels of ability and diverse interests and experiences, work together to solve a problem, complete a task, or create a product. The responsibility for learning is placed squarely on the shoulders of the students. Each student is individually accountable for their own work, and the work of the group as a whole is also evaluated. The role of the teacher is to guide and assist the students in the problem-solving process. A collaborative learning environment in the science classroom has many benefits.

**Benefits of Collaborative Learning**

- Engages students in active learning
- Encourages students to communicate openly
- Motivates students to cooperate and support each other
- Teaches respect for contributions of all members
- Prepares students for the real world

## Team Dynamics

It is important that the teacher organizes the classroom into teams. Teams should consist of three or four students, depending on the STEM activity. Fewer members may limit the diversity of ideas, skills, and approaches to problem solving.

## Assigning Roles

A successful collaborative learning experience requires a division of the workload among the members of a team. The teacher may wish to assign the role of each member of the team as follows:

- **Team Captain** is responsible for keeping the group on-task.

- **Recorder** is responsible for organizing the paperwork and creating drawings, diagrams, or illustrations as needed.

- **Materials Manager** is responsible for gathering the needed materials and supplies for the project.

- **Monitor** is responsible for keeping the work area tidy and for properly storing the project at the end of the class.

# STEM: Preparing Students for the 21st Century

Recent shifts in education are being driven by colleges and businesses demanding that high school graduates have the "21st-century skills" necessary for success in today's world. They are advocating schools teach students certain core competencies such as collaboration, critical thinking, and problem solving. STEM education focuses on these skills and, at the same time, fosters student interests in the fields of science, technology, engineering, and mathematics.

## Why STEM Education?

### STEM Promotes:
- student-centered learning.
- collaboration and teamwork.
- equality (equally benefits boys and girls).
- critical-thinking skills.
- hands-on, inquiry-based learning.
- use of technology.
- engineering design process.
- opportunities to apply math skills and knowledge.
- greater depth of subject exploration.
- innovation.
- real-world problem solving.
- curiosity and creativity.
- teachers as facilitators and monitors of learning.

## Common Hurdles to STEM Education

### STEM Requires:
- students have baseline skills in reading, math, and science to be successful.
- students be able to work well with others.
- flexible lesson plans; projects may take one class period to several weeks to complete.

# The Pieces of STEM

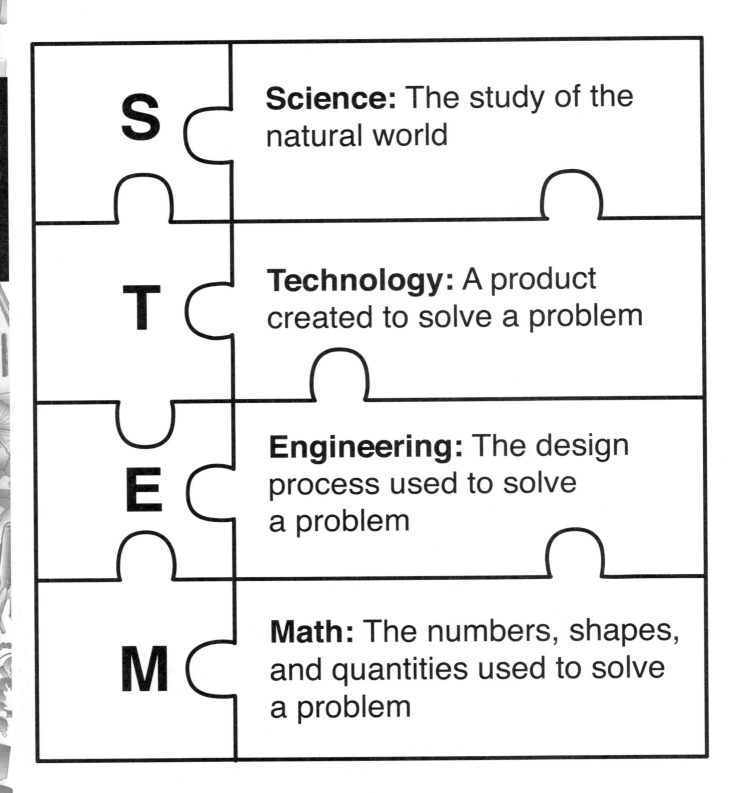

**S**

**Science:** The study of the natural world

**T**

**Technology:** A product created to solve a problem

**E**

**Engineering:** The design process used to solve a problem

**M**

**Math:** The numbers, shapes, and quantities used to solve a problem

# 10 Tips for Student Collaboration

1. Respect Each Other and All Ideas

2. No "Put Downs"

3. Be a Good, Active Listener

4. Come Well Prepared for Task Assignment

5. Participate and Contribute During Discussions

6. Support Your Opinions

7. Promote Positive Team-Member Relations

8. Disagree in an Agreeable Manner

9. Encourage Team Members

10. Complete Tasks on Time and With Quality Work

Name: _____                                                  Date: _____

# STEM Lab Challenge Rubric

| Task | 4 | 3 | 2 | 1 |
|------|---|---|---|---|
| **Research** | Demonstrates planned technological and other research/inquiry that lead to educated decisions; all information cited following copyright guidelines | Demonstrates technological and other research/inquiry; most information cited | Demonstrates some technological and other research/inquiry; some information cited | Demonstrates no technological and other research/inquiry; no information cited |
| **Model Process or System** | Drawing has labels and advanced explanation of strategy | Drawing has labels and explanation of strategy | Drawing has some labels and partial explanation of strategy | Drawing has no labels or explanation of strategy |
| **Results** | All records, analysis, and interpretation of test results in organized, accurate manner | Records, analysis, and interpretation of test results completed | Records, analysis, and/ or interpretation of test results incomplete | No records, analysis, or interpretation of test results |
| **Conclusion** | Demonstrates high-level thinking when summarizing the purpose, test procedure, and test results | Demonstrates thinking skills summarizing the purpose, test procedure, and test results | Demonstrates some thinking skills summarizing the purpose, test procedure, and test results | Demonstrates no thinking skills summarizing the purpose, test procedure, and test results |
| **Reflection** | Reflection completed with thoughtful insight into team's choices | Reflection completed with insight into team's choices | Reflection partially completed with little insight into team's choices | Reflection incomplete |
| **Evaluation** | Self-evaluation completed with thoughtful insights about behavior and performance as a team member | Self-evaluation completed with insights | Self-evaluation partially completed; some insights | Self-evaluation incomplete—no insights |

**Teacher Comments:**

Name: _____                                                                  Date: _____

# STEM Lab Self-Evaluation Rubric

**Directions:** Circle the description in each category that you believe best describes your behavior and performance during the assigned lab challenge.

| Category | 4 | 3 | 2 | 1 |
|---|---|---|---|---|
| **Attitude** | Always positive attitude about the challenge; never critical of the project or the work of other team members | Mostly positive attitude about the challenge; rarely critical of the project or the work of other team members | Usually positive attitude about challenge; sometimes critical of the project or the work of other team members | Negative attitude about challenge; often critical of the project or the work of other team members |
| **Work Quality** | Highest quality work | High quality work | Work occasionally needs to be redone by others to ensure quality | Work needs to be redone by others to ensure quality |
| **Innovative Problem-solving** | Seeks multiple, innovative solutions to the problem to meet the challenge | Seeks some innovative solutions to the problem to meet the challenge | Seeks a few possible solutions to the problem to meet the challenge | Seeks no solutions to the problem to meet the challenge |
| **Contributions** | Consistently works to fulfill challenge requirements and perform individual team-member role | Frequently works to fulfill challenge requirements and perform individual team-member role | Sometimes works to fulfill challenge requirements and perform individual team-member role | Seldom works to fulfill challenge requirements and perform individual team-member role |
| **Lab Focus** | Focuses with team members to complete the lab challenge without having to be reminded; self-directed | Focuses with team members to complete the lab challenge; rarely needs reminding; reliable team member | Sometimes focuses with team members to complete the lab challenge; often needs reminding; unreliable team member | Seldom focuses with team members to complete the lab challenge; often disruptive; unreliable team member |

**Student Comments:**

# Reflection

Name: _____ Date: _____

Title of Lab Challenge: _____

**Directions:** Complete the following statements about your lab challenge.

| | |
|---|---|
| One thing I didn't expect from this challenge was | If I want to get better at scientific investigation, I need to |
| One thing I would improve if I did this lab again would be | One thing I would like to learn more about after doing this investigation is |
| After completing this challenge, I realize that | The hardest part of this investigation was |

From completing this investigative lab, I now understand

# Walk-Through Cells: Teacher Information

## STEM Lab Overview

Students are challenged to design a large 3-dimensional model of both a plant and animal cell that other students can walk through. The parts of the cell structure and cell organelles should be labeled within each model.

## Concepts

- Animal cell
- Plant cell

## Standards for Grades 6–8

| NGSS | NCTM | ITEA | CCSS |
|---|---|---|---|
| -Structure, Function, and Information Processing | -Problem Solving<br>-Communication<br>-Connections<br>-Representation | -Nature of Technology<br>-Technology and Society<br>-Technological World | -English Language Arts Standards:<br>    Science & Technical Subjects |

## Teaching Strategies

Step #1:  Engage—Review concepts. Introduce the STEM lab. Discuss the challenge presented in the lab, providing students with an opportunity to connect previous knowledge to the problem they are to solve.

Step #2:  Investigate—Students conduct research to gain an understanding of the major science concepts related to the topic, review possible solutions to the lab challenge, and formulate new ideas for solving the problem.

Step #3:  Explore—Students apply research to design and test a model, process, or system to solve the problem presented in the challenge.

Step #4:  Communicate—Students share results.

Step #5:  Evaluate—Students are given an opportunity to reflect on what they have learned.

## Managing the Lab

- Set a deadline for project submission and presentations.
- Group students into collaborative teams and assign roles.
- Review prerequisite skills students need for doing the lab, such as measuring, weighing, constructing, recording data, graphing, and so on.
- Review science safety rules.
- Review lab cleanup procedures.
- Have the needed materials available, organized, and set up for easy access.
- Monitor teams and provide productive feedback.
- Leave enough time at the end of class for cleanup and debriefing.
- Designate area for project storage.

## Evaluation

Student Reflection: Students think about their team's choices for the design of the prototype. Students individually complete the "Reflection" handout.

Student Self-Evaluation: Students think about their behavior and performance as a team member. Students individually complete the "Self-Evaluation Rubric."

Lab Evaluation: The teacher completes the "Lab Challenge Rubric" for each team member.

Conference: Teacher/student conferences are held to discuss the completed evaluations.

Structure of Life

# Walk-Through Cells: Student Challenge

**STEM Lab Challenge:** Design a large 3-dimensional model of both a plant and animal cell that other students can walk through. The parts of the cell structure and cell organelles should be labeled within each model.

## You Should Know

All cells have three things in common. They all have a nucleus (control center for the cell), cell membrane (a thin layer that encloses the cell), and cytoplasm (a gel-like material that contains proteins, nutrients, and all of the other cell organelles).

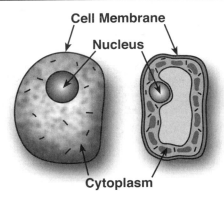

**Cell Membrane**
**Nucleus**
**Cytoplasm**
**Animal Cell**     **Plant Cell**

## Vocabulary Review
- cell membrane
- cytoplasm
- nucleus
- organelles

## Materials You May Need
- design materials: to be determined by student research

## Challenge Requirements

1. <u>Research</u>: Write a one- to two-page paper summarizing your research on plant and animal cells. Cite your sources. Your paper may include two pictures.
2. <u>Model</u>: Label a drawing of each of your cell designs and explain your strategy.
3. <u>Results</u>: Record, analyze, and interpret test results.
4. <u>Conclusion</u>: Summarize the lab and what actually happened. It should include the purpose, a brief description of the test procedure, and explanation of results.
5. <u>Reflection</u>: Think about your team's choices for each cell design. Then complete the "Reflection" handout.
6. <u>Evaluation</u>: Think about your behavior and performance as a team member. Then complete the "Self-Evaluation Rubric."

## Steps to Follow

*Work with a team to complete the steps listed below. A team will have 3 or 4 members.*

Step 1: Research plant and animal cells.
Step 2: Brainstorm ideas about how to design a walk-through plant and animal cell to meet the requirements of the lab.
Step 3: Draw a diagram of each design.
Step 4: Construct the two cell models.
Step 5: Test the accuracy of the models by using your science book or other resources. Record the results of your comparisons.
Step 6: Evaluate how well the items chosen for your cell models represent the actual parts of each cell.
Step 7: Identify how to improve both of your designs.
Step 8: Make the needed changes.
Step 9: Retest and reevaluate the improved designs.
Step 10: Share the results.

# Mitosis Model: Teacher Information

## STEM Lab Overview

Students are challenged to design a model of mitosis that illustrates the phases in the process of cell division.

## Concepts

- Mitosis
- Cell cycle

## Standards for Grades 6–8

| NGSS | NCTM | ITEA | CCSS |
|------|------|------|------|
| -Structure, Function, and Information Processing | -Problem Solving<br>-Communication<br>-Connections<br>-Representation | -Nature of Technology<br>-Technology and Society<br>-Technological World | -English Language Arts Standards:<br>　Science & Technical Subjects |

## Teaching Strategies

Step #1:  Engage—Review concepts. Introduce the STEM lab. Discuss the challenge presented in the lab, providing students with an opportunity to connect previous knowledge to the problem they are to solve.

Step #2:  Investigate—Students conduct research to gain an understanding of the major science concepts related to the topic, review possible solutions to the lab challenge, and formulate new ideas for solving the problem.

Step #3:  Explore—Students apply research to design and test a model, process, or system to solve the problem presented in the challenge.

Step #4:  Communicate—Students share results.

Step #5:  Evaluate—Students are given an opportunity to reflect on what they have learned.

## Managing the Lab

- Set a deadline for project submission and presentations.
- Group students into collaborative teams and assign roles.
- Review prerequisite skills students need for doing the lab, such as measuring, weighing, constructing, recording data, graphing, and so on.
- Review science safety rules.
- Review lab cleanup procedures.
- Have the needed materials available, organized, and set up for easy access.
- Monitor teams and provide productive feedback.
- Leave enough time at the end of class for cleanup and debriefing.
- Designate area for project storage.

## Evaluation

Student Reflection: Students think about their team's choices for the design of the prototype. Students individually complete the "Reflection" handout.

Student Self-Evaluation: Students think about their behavior and performance as a team member. Students individually complete the "Self-Evaluation Rubric."

Lab Evaluation: The teacher completes the "Lab Challenge Rubric" for each team member.

Conference: Teacher/student conferences are held to discuss the completed evaluations.

# Mitosis Model: Student Challenge

**STEM Lab Challenge:** Design a model of mitosis that illustrates the phases in the process of cell division.

## You Should Know

All living things grow and repair themselves by the process of mitosis. During this process, one cell divides to form two identical cells, or daughter cells.

**Two Daughter Cells Forming**

## Vocabulary Review

- daughter cells
- chromosome
- mitosis
- nucleus
- parent cell

## Materials You May Need

- design materials: to be determined by student research

## Challenge Requirements

1. Research: Write a one- to two-page paper summarizing your research on the process of mitosis. Cite your sources. Your paper may include two pictures.
2. Model: Label a drawing of your mitosis model and explain your strategy.
3. Results: Record, analyze, and interpret test results.
4. Conclusion: Summarize the lab and what actually happened. It should include the purpose, a brief description of the test procedure, and explanation of results.
5. Reflection: Think about your team's choices for the mitosis model. Then complete the "Reflection" handout.
6. Evaluation: Think about your behavior and performance as a team member. Then complete the "Self-Evaluation Rubric."

## Steps to Follow

*Work with a team to complete the steps listed below. A team will have 3 or 4 members.*

Step 1: Research the process of mitosis.
Step 2: Brainstorm ideas about how to design a model of the process of mitosis to meet the requirements of the lab.
Step 3: Draw a diagram of your design.
Step 4: Construct the model.
Step 5: Test the accuracy of the model by using your science book or other resources. Record the results of your comparisons.
Step 6: Evaluate how well the items chosen for your model actually represent the five phases in the process of mitosis.
Step 7: Identify how to improve your design.
Step 8: Make the needed changes.
Step 9: Retest and reevaluate the improved design.
Step 10: Share the results.

# Osmosis: Teacher Information

## STEM Lab Overview

Students are challenged to design a model to demonstrate the process of osmosis in cells.

## Concepts

- Cell processes
- Osmosis

## Standards for Grades 6–8

| NGSS | NCTM | ITEA | CCSS |
|---|---|---|---|
| -Growth, Development, and Reproduction of Organisms | -Problem Solving<br>-Communication<br>-Connections<br>-Representation | -Nature of Technology<br>-Technology and Society<br>-Technological World | -English Language Arts Standards:<br>Science & Technical Subjects |

## Teaching Strategies

Step #1:  Engage—Review concepts. Introduce the STEM lab. Discuss the challenge presented in the lab, providing students with an opportunity to connect previous knowledge to the problem they are to solve.

Step #2:  Investigate—Students conduct research to gain an understanding of the major science concepts related to the topic, review possible solutions to the lab challenge, and formulate new ideas for solving the problem.

Step #3:  Explore—Students apply research to design and test a model, process, or system to solve the problem presented in the challenge.

Step #4:  Communicate—Students share results.

Step #5:  Evaluate—Students are given an opportunity to reflect on what they have learned.

## Managing the Lab

- Set a deadline for project submission and presentations.
- Group students into collaborative teams and assign roles.
- Review prerequisite skills students need for doing the lab, such as measuring, weighing, constructing, recording data, graphing, and so on.
- Review science safety rules.
- Review lab cleanup procedures.
- Have the needed materials available, organized, and set up for easy access.
- Monitor teams and provide productive feedback.
- Leave enough time at the end of class for cleanup and debriefing.
- Designate area for project storage.

## Evaluation

Student Reflection: Students think about their team's choices for the design of the prototype. Students individually complete the "Reflection" handout.

Student Self-Evaluation: Students think about their behavior and performance as a team member. Students individually complete the "Self-Evaluation Rubric."

Lab Evaluation: The teacher completes the "Lab Challenge Rubric" for each team member.

Conference: Teacher/student conferences are held to discuss the completed evaluations.

# Osmosis: Student Challenge

**STEM Lab Challenge:** Design a working model to demonstrate the process of osmosis in cells.

## You Should Know

The cell membrane controls what enters and leaves a cell. To carry on life processes, oxygen, food, and water molecules must pass through the cell's membrane, and waste products must be removed from the cell through the membrane.

### Osmosis in Plant Cells

Low water concentration outside the cell

Equal water concentrations inside and out

High water concentration outside the cell

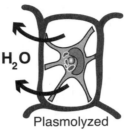
$H_2O$  $H_2O$
Plasmolyzed

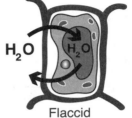
$H_2O$  $H_2O$
Flaccid

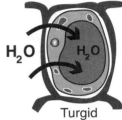
$H_2O$  $H_2O$
Turgid

## Vocabulary Review

- diffusion
- osmosis
- molecules

## Materials You May Need

- design materials: to be determined by student research

## Challenge Requirements

1. <u>Research</u>: Write a one- to two-page paper summarizing your research on cell processes and osmosis. Cite your sources. Your paper may include two pictures.
2. <u>Model</u>: Label a drawing of your osmosis model and explain your strategy.
3. <u>Results</u>: Record, analyze, and interpret test results.
4. <u>Conclusion</u>: Summarize the lab and what actually happened. It should include the purpose, a brief description of the test procedure, and explanation of results.
5. <u>Reflection</u>: Think about your team's choices for the osmosis model. Then complete the "Reflection" handout.
6. <u>Evaluation</u>: Think about your behavior and performance as a team member. Then complete the "Self-Evaluation Rubric."

## Steps to Follow

*Work with a team to complete the steps listed below. A team will have 3 or 4 members.*

Step 1: Research cell processes and osmosis.
Step 2: Brainstorm ideas about how you might make an osmosis model to meet the requirements of the lab.
Step 3: Draw a diagram of your model.
Step 4: Construct your osmosis model.
Step 5: Test the design and record the results.
Step 6: Evaluate the performance of your osmosis model.
Step 7: Identify how to improve your design.
Step 8: Make the needed changes.
Step 9: Retest and reevaluate the design.
Step 10: Share the results.

# The Human Skeletal System: Teacher Information

## STEM Lab Overview

Students are challenged to design a life-like model of the human skeletal system using everyday materials.

## Concepts

• Skeletal system

## Standards for Grades 6–8

| NGSS | NCTM | ITEA | CCSS |
|---|---|---|---|
| -Growth, Development, and Reproduction of Organisms | -Problem Solving<br>-Communication<br>-Connections<br>-Representation | -Nature of Technology<br>-Technology and Society<br>-Technological World | -English Language Arts Standards:<br>    Science & Technical Subjects |

## Teaching Strategies

Step #1:   Engage—Review concepts. Introduce the STEM lab. Discuss the challenge presented in the lab, providing students with an opportunity to connect previous knowledge to the problem they are to solve.

Step #2:   Investigate—Students conduct research to gain an understanding of the major science concepts related to the topic, review possible solutions to the lab challenge, and formulate new ideas for solving the problem.

Step #3:   Explore—Students apply research to design and test a model, process, or system to solve the problem presented in the challenge.

Step #4:   Communicate—Students share results.

Step #5:   Evaluate—Students are given an opportunity to reflect on what they have learned.

## Managing the Lab

• Set a deadline for project submission and presentations.
• Group students into collaborative teams and assign roles.
• Review prerequisite skills students need for doing the lab, such as measuring, weighing, constructing, recording data, graphing, and so on.
• Review science safety rules.
• Review lab cleanup procedures.
• Have the needed materials available, organized, and set up for easy access.
• Monitor teams and provide productive feedback.
• Leave enough time at the end of class for cleanup and debriefing.
• Designate area for project storage.

## Evaluation

Student Reflection: Students think about their team's choices for the design of the prototype. Students individually complete the "Reflection" handout.

Student Self-Evaluation: Students think about their behavior and performance as a team member. Students individually complete the "Self-Evaluation Rubric."

Lab Evaluation: The teacher completes the "Lab Challenge Rubric" for each team member.

Conference: Teacher/student conferences are held to discuss the completed evaluations.

# The Human Skeletal System: Student Challenge

**STEM Lab Challenge:** Design a life-like model of the human skeletal system using everyday materials.

## Vocabulary Review

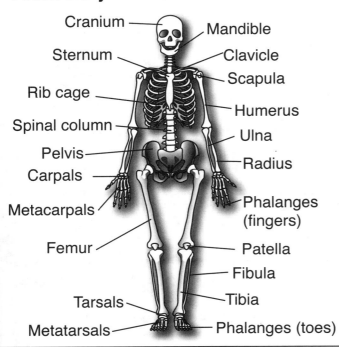

Cranium — Mandible
Sternum — Clavicle
— Scapula
Rib cage — Humerus
Spinal column — Ulna
Pelvis — Radius
Carpals —
Metacarpals — Phalanges (fingers)
Femur — Patella
— Fibula
Tarsals — Tibia
Metatarsals — Phalanges (toes)

## Challenge Requirements

1. <u>Research</u>: Write a one- to two-page paper summarizing your research on the skeletal system. Cite your sources. Your paper may include two pictures.
2. <u>Model</u>: Label a drawing of your skeletal system model and explain your strategy.
3. <u>Results</u>: Record, analyze, and interpret test results.
4. <u>Conclusion</u>: Summarize the lab and what actually happened. It should include the purpose, a brief description of the test procedure, and explanation of results.
5. <u>Reflection</u>: Think about your team's choices for the parts of your skeleton model. Then complete the "Reflection" handout.
6. <u>Evaluation</u>: Think about your behavior and performance as a team member. Then complete the "Self-Evaluation Rubric."

## You Should Know

The human skeleton is made up of approximately 206 individual bones.

## Materials You May Need

- design materials: to be determined by student research

## Steps to Follow

*Work with a team to complete the steps listed below. A team will have 3 or 4 members.*

Step 1: Research the skeletal system.
Step 2: Brainstorm ideas about how you might design a life-like skeleton to meet the requirements of the lab. Focus on the size, shape, and appearance of the bones.
Step 3: Draw a diagram of your skeletal system model.
Step 4: Construct the model.
Step 5: Test the accuracy of the model by using your science book or other resources. Record the results of your comparisons.
Step 6: Evaluate how well the items chosen for your model actually represent the parts of the skeletal system.
Step 7: Identify how to improve the design.
Step 8: Make the needed changes.
Step 9: Test and reevaluate the improved design.
Step 10: Share the results.

# Biceps and Triceps: Teacher Information

## STEM Lab Overview

Students are challenged to design a model of the arm that demonstrates how the biceps and triceps muscles work.

## Concepts

- Muscular system
- biceps and triceps

## Standards for Grades 6–8

| NGSS | NCTM | ITEA | CCSS |
|------|------|------|------|
| -Growth, Development, and Reproduction of Organisms | -Problem Solving<br>-Communication<br>-Connections<br>-Representation | -Nature of Technology<br>-Technology and Society<br>-Technological World | -English Language Arts Standards:<br>Science & Technical Subjects |

## Teaching Strategies

Step #1: Engage—Review concepts. Introduce the STEM lab. Discuss the challenge presented in the lab, providing students with an opportunity to connect previous knowledge to the problem they are to solve.

Step #2: Investigate—Students conduct research to gain an understanding of the major science concepts related to the topic, review possible solutions to the lab challenge, and formulate new ideas for solving the problem.

Step #3: Explore—Students apply research to design and test a model, process, or system to solve the problem presented in the challenge.

Step #4: Communicate—Students share results.

Step #5: Evaluate—Students are given an opportunity to reflect on what they have learned.

## Managing the Lab

- Set a deadline for project submission and presentations.
- Group students into collaborative teams and assign roles.
- Review prerequisite skills students need for doing the lab, such as measuring, weighing, constructing, recording data, graphing, and so on.
- Review science safety rules.
- Review lab cleanup procedures.
- Have the needed materials available, organized, and set up for easy access.
- Monitor teams and provide productive feedback.
- Leave enough time at the end of class for cleanup and debriefing.
- Designate area for project storage.

## Evaluation

Student Reflection: Students think about their team's choices for the design of the prototype. Students individually complete the "Reflection" handout.

Student Self-Evaluation: Students think about their behavior and performance as a team member. Students individually complete the "Self-Evaluation Rubric."

Lab Evaluation: The teacher completes the "Lab Challenge Rubric" for each team member.

Conference: Teacher/student conferences are held to discuss the completed evaluations.

Human Body Systems

# Biceps and Triceps: Student Challenge

**STEM Lab Challenge:** Design a model of the arm that demonstrates how the biceps and triceps muscles work.

## You Should Know
Your muscular system works along with your skeletal system to help you move.

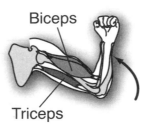

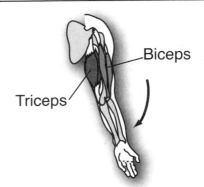

## Vocabulary Review
- biceps
- muscular system
- skeletal muscle
- triceps

## Materials You May Need
- design materials: to be determined by student research

## Challenge Requirements
1. <u>Research</u>: Write a one- to two-page paper summarizing your research on the muscular system and the biceps and triceps muscles. Cite your sources. Your paper may include two pictures.
2. <u>Model</u>: Label a drawing of your arm model and explain your strategy.
3. <u>Results</u>: Record, analyze, and interpret test results.
4. <u>Conclusion</u>: Summarize the lab and what actually happened. It should include the purpose, a brief description of the test procedure, and explanation of results.
5. <u>Reflection</u>: Think about your team's choices for the arm model. Then complete the "Reflection" handout.
6. <u>Evaluation</u>: Think about your behavior and performance as a team member. Then complete the "Self-Evaluation Rubric."

## Steps to Follow
*Work with a team to complete the steps listed below. A team will have 3 or 4 members.*

Step 1:   Research the muscular system and the biceps and triceps muscles.
Step 2:   Brainstorm ideas about how to design an arm model to meet the requirements of the lab. One muscle of the model should stretch and the other should get shorter when you bend and straighten the arm.
Step 3:   Draw a diagram of your design.
Step 4:   Construct the model.
Step 5:   Test your model and record the results.
Step 6:   Evaluate how well the items chosen for your model actually represent the parts of the arm.
Step 7:   Identify how to improve your design.
Step 8:   Make the needed changes.
Step 9:   Retest and reevaluate the improved design.
Step 10: Share the results.

# Circulatory System: Teacher Information

## STEM Lab Overview

Students are challenged to design a working model of the human circulatory system that simulates the flow of blood.

## Concepts

• Circulatory system

## Standards for Grades 6–8

| NGSS | NCTM | ITEA | CCSS |
|---|---|---|---|
| -Growth, Development, and Reproduction of Organisms | -Problem Solving<br>-Communication<br>-Connections<br>-Representation | -Nature of Technology<br>-Technology and Society<br>-Technological World | -English Language Arts Standards:<br>  Science & Technical Subjects |

## Teaching Strategies

Step #1:   Engage—Review concepts. Introduce the STEM lab. Discuss the challenge presented in the lab, providing students with an opportunity to connect previous knowledge to the problem they are to solve.

Step #2:   Investigate—Students conduct research to gain an understanding of the major science concepts related to the topic, review possible solutions to the lab challenge, and formulate new ideas for solving the problem.

Step #3:   Explore—Students apply research to design and test a model, process, or system to solve the problem presented in the challenge.

Step #4:   Communicate—Students share results.

Step #5:   Evaluate—Students are given an opportunity to reflect on what they have learned.

## Managing the Lab

• Set a deadline for project submission and presentations.
• Group students into collaborative teams and assign roles.
• Review prerequisite skills students need for doing the lab, such as measuring, weighing, constructing, recording data, graphing, and so on.
• Review science safety rules.
• Review lab cleanup procedures.
• Have the needed materials available, organized, and set up for easy access.
• Monitor teams and provide productive feedback.
• Leave enough time at the end of class for cleanup and debriefing.
• Designate area for project storage.

## Evaluation

Student Reflection: Students think about their team's choices for the design of the prototype. Students individually complete the "Reflection" handout.

Student Self-Evaluation: Students think about their behavior and performance as a team member. Students individually complete the "Self-Evaluation Rubric."

Lab Evaluation: The teacher completes the "Lab Challenge Rubric" for each team member.

Conference: Teacher/student conferences are held to discuss the completed evaluations.

# Circulatory System: Student Challenge

**STEM Lab Challenge:** Design a working model of the human circulatory system that simulates the flow of blood.

## You Should Know

The circulatory system transports needed substances through your body and carries away wastes.

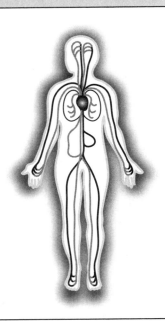

## Vocabulary Review
- arteries
- blood
- blood vessels
- capillaries
- circulatory system
- heart
- veins

## Materials You May Need
- design materials: to be determined by student research

## Challenge Requirements

1. <u>Research</u>: Write a one- to two-page paper summarizing your research on the human heart and circulatory system. Cite your sources. Your paper may include two pictures.
2. <u>Model</u>: Label a drawing of your circulatory system model and explain your strategy.
3. <u>Results</u>: Record, analyze, and interpret test results.
4. <u>Conclusion</u>: Summarize the lab and what actually happened. It should include the purpose, a brief description of the test procedure, and explanation of results.
5. <u>Reflection</u>: Think about your team's choices for the circulatory system model. Then complete the "Reflection" handout.
6. <u>Evaluation</u>: Think about your behavior and performance as a team member. Then complete the "Self-Evaluation Rubric."

## Steps to Follow

*Work with a team to complete the steps listed below. A team will have 3 or 4 members.*

Step 1: Research the human heart and circulatory system.

Step 2: Brainstorm ideas about how you might design a model of the human circulatory system to meet the requirements of the lab. Think about what materials you could use for the different parts of the system.

Step 3: Draw a diagram of your model.

Step 4: Construct your model.

Step 5: Test the design and record the results.

Step 6: Evaluate the performance of your circulatory system model.

Step 7: Identify how to improve your design.

Step 8: Make the needed changes.

Step 9: Retest and reevaluate the design.

Step 10: Share the results.

# How the Lungs and Diaphragm Work: Teacher Information

## STEM Lab Overview

Students are challenged to design a working model of the human lungs and diaphragm. Students should be able to explain the parts of the model as they demonstrate how it works.

## Concepts

- Respiratory system

## Standards for Grades 6–8

| NGSS | NCTM | ITEA | CCSS |
|---|---|---|---|
| -Growth, Development, and Reproduction of Organisms | -Problem Solving<br>-Communication<br>-Connections<br>-Representation | -Nature of Technology<br>-Technology and Society<br>-Technological World | -English Language Arts Standards:<br>Science & Technical Subjects |

## Teaching Strategies

Step #1:   Engage—Review concepts. Introduce the STEM lab. Discuss the challenge presented in the lab, providing students with an opportunity to connect previous knowledge to the problem they are to solve.

Step #2:   Investigate—Students conduct research to gain an understanding of the major science concepts related to the topic, review possible solutions to the lab challenge, and formulate new ideas for solving the problem.

Step #3:   Explore—Students apply research to design and test a model, process, or system to solve the problem presented in the challenge.

Step #4:   Communicate—Students share results.

Step #5:   Evaluate—Students are given an opportunity to reflect on what they have learned.

## Managing the Lab

- Set a deadline for project submission and presentations.
- Group students into collaborative teams and assign roles.
- Review prerequisite skills students need for doing the lab, such as measuring, weighing, constructing, recording data, graphing, and so on.
- Review science safety rules.
- Review lab cleanup procedures.
- Have the needed materials available, organized, and set up for easy access.
- Monitor teams and provide productive feedback.
- Leave enough time at the end of class for cleanup and debriefing.
- Designate area for project storage.

## Evaluation

Student Reflection: Students think about their team's choices for the design of the prototype. Students individually complete the "Reflection" handout.

Student Self-Evaluation: Students think about their behavior and performance as a team member. Students individually complete the "Self-Evaluation Rubric."

Lab Evaluation: The teacher completes the "Lab Challenge Rubric" for each team member.

Conference: Teacher/student conferences are held to discuss the completed evaluations.

Human Body Systems

# How the Lungs and Diaphragm Work: Student Challenge

**STEM Lab Challenge:** Design a working model of the human lungs and diaphragm. You should be able to explain the parts of the model as you demonstrate how it works.

## You Should Know
Your lungs and diaphragm are part of your respiratory system. The diaphragm, and other muscles, help your lungs expand and contract so you can inhale and exhale.

## Vocabulary Review
- alveoli
- bronchi
- capillaries
- diaphragm
- larynx
- lungs
- pharynx
- rib cage
- trachea

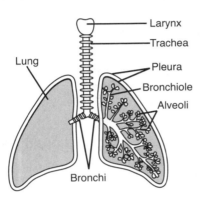

## Materials You May Need
- two-liter plastic bottle
- soda straws
- rubber bands
- balloons
- scissors
- plastic bags
- modeling compound
- masking tape
- other design materials: to be determined by student research

## Challenge Requirements
1. Research: Write a one- to two-page paper summarizing your research on the human respiratory system. Cite your sources. Your paper may include two pictures.
2. Model: Label a drawing of your lung and diaphragm model and explain your strategy.
3. Results: Record, analyze, and interpret test results.
4. Conclusion: Summarize the lab and what actually happened. It should include the purpose, a brief description of the test procedure, and explanation of results.
5. Reflection: Think about your team's choices for the lung and diaphragm model. Then complete the "Reflection" handout.
6. Evaluation: Think about your behavior and performance as a team member. Then complete the "Self-Evaluation Rubric."

## Steps to Follow
*Work with a team to complete the steps listed below. A team will have 3 or 4 members.*

Step 1:  Research the human respiratory system.
Step 2:  Brainstorm ideas about how to design a lung and diaphragm model to meet the requirements of the lab.
Step 3:  Draw a diagram of your design.
Step 4:  Construct the model.
Step 5:  Test the accuracy of the model by using your science book or other resources. Record the results of your comparisons.
Step 6:  Evaluate how well the items chosen for your model actually represent the parts of the lungs and diaphragm.
Step 7:  Identify how to improve your design.
Step 8:  Make the needed changes.
Step 9:  Retest and reevaluate the improved design.
Step 10: Share the results.

# The Human Digestive System: Teacher Information

## STEM Lab Overview

Students are challenged to design a working model of the human digestive system. The food journey steps should be labeled and include a brief explanation.

## Concepts

- Digestive system
- Excretory system

## Standards for Grades 6–8

| NGSS | NCTM | ITEA | CCSS |
|---|---|---|---|
| -Growth, Development, and Reproduction of Organisms | -Problem Solving<br>-Communication<br>-Connections<br>-Representation | -Nature of Technology<br>-Technology and Society<br>-Technological World | -English Language Arts Standards:<br>  Science & Technical Subjects |

## Teaching Strategies

Step #1:  Engage—Review concepts. Introduce the STEM lab. Discuss the challenge presented in the lab, providing students with an opportunity to connect previous knowledge to the problem they are to solve.

Step #2:  Investigate—Students conduct research to gain an understanding of the major science concepts related to the topic, review possible solutions to the lab challenge, and formulate new ideas for solving the problem.

Step #3:  Explore—Students apply research to design and test a model, process, or system to solve the problem presented in the challenge.

Step #4:  Communicate—Students share results.

Step #5:  Evaluate—Students are given an opportunity to reflect on what they have learned.

## Managing the Lab

- Set a deadline for project submission and presentations.
- Group students into collaborative teams and assign roles.
- Review prerequisite skills students need for doing the lab, such as measuring, weighing, constructing, recording data, graphing, and so on.
- Review science safety rules.
- Review lab cleanup procedures.
- Have the needed materials available, organized, and set up for easy access.
- Monitor teams and provide productive feedback.
- Leave enough time at the end of class for cleanup and debriefing.
- Designate area for project storage.

## Evaluation

Student Reflection: Students think about their team's choices for the design of the prototype. Students individually complete the "Reflection" handout.

Student Self-Evaluation: Students think about their behavior and performance as a team member. Students individually complete the "Self-Evaluation Rubric."

Lab Evaluation: The teacher completes the "Lab Challenge Rubric" for each team member.

Conference: Teacher/student conferences are held to discuss the completed evaluations.

# The Human Digestive System: Student Challenge

**STEM Lab Challenge:** Design a working model of the human digestive system. The food journey steps should be labeled and include a brief explanation.

## You Should Know
The job of the digestive system is to break food down into substances the body can use.

## Vocabulary Review
- anus
- enzymes
- esophagus
- gall bladder
- large intestine
- liver
- mouth
- pancreas
- rectum
- small intestine
- stomach

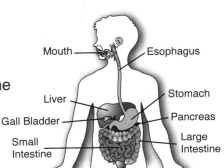

Mouth — Esophagus — Liver — Stomach — Gall Bladder — Pancreas — Small Intestine — Large Intestine — Anus — Rectum

## Materials You May Need
- duct tape
- scissors
- pantyhose
- rubber glove or quart-size baggie
- spoon
- long balloon
- sandwich bag clips or strong clothes pins
- plastic funnel
- water, banana, and saltine crackers
- other design materials: to be determined by student research

## Challenge Requirements
1. <u>Research</u>: Write a one- to two-page paper summarizing your research on the human digestive system. Cite your sources. Your paper may include two pictures.
2. <u>Model</u>: Label a drawing of your human digestive system model and explain your strategy.
3. <u>Results</u>: Record, analyze, and interpret test results.
4. <u>Conclusion</u>: Summarize the lab and what actually happened. It should include the purpose, a brief description of the test procedure, and explanation of results.
5. <u>Reflection</u>: Think about your team's choices for the human digestive system model. Then complete the "Reflection" handout.
6. <u>Evaluation</u>: Think about your behavior and performance as a team member. Then complete the "Self-Evaluation Rubric."

## Steps to Follow
*Work with a team to complete the steps listed below. A team will have 3 or 4 members.*

Step 1: Research the human digestive system.
Step 2: Brainstorm ideas about how to design a digestive system to meet the requirements of the lab.
Step 3: Draw a diagram of your design.
Step 4: Construct and label the model.
Step 5: Test the accuracy of your model. Record the results.
Step 6: Evaluate how well the items chosen for your model actually represent the parts of the digestive system.
Step 7: Identify how to improve your design.
Step 8: Make the needed changes.
Step 9: Retest and reevaluate the improved design.
Step 10: Share the results.

# The Brain: Teacher Information

## STEM Lab Overview

Students are challenged to design a 3-dimensional model of the human brain. The model should contain the major parts of the brain. Each part should be labeled and include a brief description of its function.

## Concepts to Review

- Brain
- Central nervous system

## Standards for Grades 6–8

| NGSS | NCTM | ITEA | CCSS |
|---|---|---|---|
| -Structure, Function, and Information Processing | -Problem Solving<br>-Communication<br>-Connections<br>-Representation | -Nature of Technology<br>-Technology and Society<br>-Technological World | -English Language Arts Standards:<br>Science & Technical Subjects |

## Teaching Strategies

Step #1: Engage—Review concepts. Introduce the STEM lab. Discuss the challenge presented in the lab, providing students with an opportunity to connect previous knowledge to the problem they are to solve.

Step #2: Investigate—Students conduct research to gain an understanding of the major science concepts related to the topic, review possible solutions to the lab challenge, and formulate new ideas for solving the problem.

Step #3: Explore—Students apply research to design and test a model, process, or system to solve the problem presented in the challenge.

Step #4: Communicate—Students share results.

Step #5: Evaluate—Students are given an opportunity to reflect on what they have learned.

## Managing the Lab

- Set a deadline for project submission and presentations.
- Group students into collaborative teams and assign roles.
- Review prerequisite skills students need for doing the lab, such as measuring, weighing, constructing, recording data, graphing, and so on.
- Review science safety rules.
- Review lab cleanup procedures.
- Have the needed materials available, organized, and set up for easy access.
- Monitor teams and provide productive feedback.
- Leave enough time at the end of class for cleanup and debriefing.
- Designate area for project storage.

## Evaluation

Student Reflection: Students think about their team's choices for the design of the prototype. Students individually complete the "Reflection" handout.

Student Self-Evaluation: Students think about their behavior and performance as a team member. Students individually complete the "Self-Evaluation Rubric."

Lab Evaluation: The teacher completes the "Lab Challenge Rubric" for each team member.

Conference: Teacher/student conferences are held to discuss the completed evaluations.

# The Brain: Student Challenge

**STEM Lab Challenge:** Design a 3-dimensional model of the human brain. The model should contain the major parts of the brain. Each part should be labeled and include a brief description of its function.

## You Should Know

Your brain is the center of your nervous system. It controls your thoughts, movements, memories, and decisions. Scientists are still trying to understand all of its complicated and interesting properties.

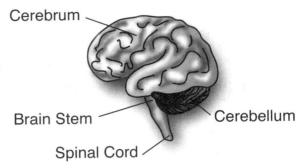

Cerebrum

Brain Stem

Cerebellum

Spinal Cord

## Vocabulary Review

- brain stem
- cerebellum
- cerebrum
- hypothalamus
- spinal cord
- central nervous system
- cerebral cortex
- hippocampus
- thalamus

## Materials You May Need

- design materials: to be determined by student research

## Challenge Requirements

1. Research: Write a one- to two-page paper summarizing your research on the human brain and brain functions. Cite your sources. Your paper may include two pictures.
2. Model: Label a drawing of your brain model and explain your strategy.
3. Results: Record, analyze, and interpret test results.
4. Conclusion: Summarize the lab and what actually happened. It should include the purpose, a brief description of the test procedure, and explanation of results.
5. Reflection: Think about your team's choices for the brain model. Then complete the "Reflection" handout.
6. Evaluation: Think about your behavior and performance as a team member. Then complete the "Self-Evaluation Rubric."

## Steps to Follow

*Work with a team to complete the steps listed below. A team will have 3 or 4 members.*

Step 1: Research the human brain and brain functions.

Step 2: Brainstorm ideas about how to design a brain model to meet the requirements of the lab.

Step 3: Draw a diagram of your design.

Step 4: Construct the model.

Step 5: Test the accuracy of the model by using your science book or other resources. Record the results of your comparisons.

Step 6: Evaluate how well the items chosen for your model actually represent the parts of the brain.

Step 7: Identify how to improve the design.

Step 8: Make the needed changes.

Step 9: Reevaluate the improved design.

Step 10: Share the results.

# The Human Eye: Teacher Information

## STEM Lab Overview

Students are challenged to design a 3-dimensional model of the human eye. The model should contain the major parts of the eye. Each part should be labeled and include a brief description of its function.

## Concepts

- Vision
- Light

## Standards for Grades 6–8

| NGSS | NCTM | ITEA | CCSS |
|------|------|------|------|
| -Growth, Development, and Reproduction of Organisms | -Problem Solving<br>-Communication<br>-Connections<br>-Representation | -Nature of Technology<br>-Technology and Society<br>-Technological World | -English Language Arts Standards:<br>    Science & Technical Subjects |

## Teaching Strategies

Step #1:   Engage—Review concepts. Introduce the STEM lab. Discuss the challenge presented in the lab, providing students with an opportunity to connect previous knowledge to the problem they are to solve.

Step #2:   Investigate—Students conduct research to gain an understanding of the major science concepts related to the topic, review possible solutions to the lab challenge, and formulate new ideas for solving the problem.

Step #3:   Explore—Students apply research to design and test a model, process, or system to solve the problem presented in the challenge.

Step #4:   Communicate—Students share results.

Step #5:   Evaluate—Students are given an opportunity to reflect on what they have learned.

## Managing the Lab

- Set a deadline for project submission and presentations.
- Group students into collaborative teams and assign roles.
- Review prerequisite skills students need for doing the lab, such as measuring, weighing, constructing, recording data, graphing, and so on.
- Review science safety rules.
- Review lab cleanup procedures.
- Have the needed materials available, organized, and set up for easy access.
- Monitor teams and provide productive feedback.
- Leave enough time at the end of class for cleanup and debriefing.
- Designate area for project storage.

## Evaluation

Student Reflection: Students think about their team's choices for the design of the prototype. Students individually complete the "Reflection" handout.

Student Self-Evaluation: Students think about their behavior and performance as a team member. Students individually complete the "Self-Evaluation Rubric."

Lab Evaluation: The teacher completes the "Lab Challenge Rubric" for each team member.

Conference: Teacher/student conferences are held to discuss the completed evaluations.

Human Body Systems

# The Human Eye: Student Challenge

**STEM Lab Challenge:** Design a 3-dimensional model of the human eye. The model should contain the major parts of the eye. Each part should be labeled and include a brief description of its function.

## You Should Know

Sight is one of the five senses that help us process information in the world around us. Our eyes are organs that detect light and allow us to see.

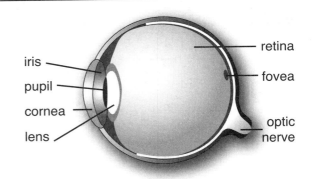

## Vocabulary Review

- cones
- iris
- optic nerve
- retina
- sclera
- cornea
- lens
- pupil
- rods

## Materials You May Need

- design materials: to be determined by student research

## Challenge Requirements

1. Research: Write a one- to two-page paper summarizing your research on vision and parts of the eye. Cite your sources. Your paper may include two pictures.
2. Model: Label a drawing of your human eye model and explain your strategy.
3. Results: Record, analyze, and interpret test results.
4. Conclusion: Summarize the lab and what actually happened. It should include the purpose, a brief description of the test procedure, and explanation of results.
5. Reflection: Think about your team's choices for the eye model. Then complete the "Reflection" handout.
6. Evaluation: Think about your behavior and performance as a team member. Then complete the "Self-Evaluation Rubric."

## Steps to Follow

*Work with a team to complete the steps listed below. A team will have 3 or 4 members.*

Step 1: Research vision and parts of the eye.
Step 2: Brainstorm ideas about how to design a human eye model to meet the requirements of the lab.
Step 3: Draw a diagram of your design.
Step 4: Construct the model.
Step 5: Test the accuracy of the model by using your science book or other resources. Record the results of your comparisons.
Step 6: Evaluate how well the items chosen for your model actually represent the parts of the eye.
Step 7: Identify how to improve your design.
Step 8: Make the needed changes.
Step 9: Retest and reevaluate the improved design.
Step 10: Share the results.

# Our Skin: Teacher Information

## STEM Lab Overview

Students are challenged to design a 3-dimensional model of human skin. The model should contain the major parts of the skin. Each part should be labeled and include a brief description of its function.

## Concepts

- Integumentary system

## Standards for Grades 6–8

| NGSS | NCTM | ITEA | CCSS |
|---|---|---|---|
| -Growth, Development, and Reproduction of Organisms | -Problem Solving<br>-Communication<br>-Connections<br>-Representation | -Nature of Technology<br>-Technology and Society<br>-Technological World | -English Language Arts Standards:<br>  Science & Technical Subjects |

## Teaching Strategies

Step #1:  Engage—Review concepts. Introduce the STEM lab. Discuss the challenge presented in the lab, providing students with an opportunity to connect previous knowledge to the problem they are to solve.

Step #2:  Investigate—Students conduct research to gain an understanding of the major science concepts related to the topic, review possible solutions to the lab challenge, and formulate new ideas for solving the problem.

Step #3:  Explore—Students apply research to design and test a model, process, or system to solve the problem presented in the challenge.

Step #4:  Communicate—Students share results.

Step #5:  Evaluate—Students are given an opportunity to reflect on what they have learned.

## Managing the Lab

- Set a deadline for project submission and presentations.
- Group students into collaborative teams and assign roles.
- Review prerequisite skills students need for doing the lab, such as measuring, weighing, constructing, recording data, graphing, and so on.
- Review science safety rules.
- Review lab cleanup procedures.
- Have the needed materials available, organized, and set up for easy access.
- Monitor teams and provide productive feedback.
- Leave enough time at the end of class for cleanup and debriefing.
- Designate area for project storage.

## Evaluation

Student Reflection: Students think about their team's choices for the design of the prototype. Students individually complete the "Reflection" handout.

Student Self-Evaluation: Students think about their behavior and performance as a team member. Students individually complete the "Self-Evaluation Rubric."

Lab Evaluation: The teacher completes the "Lab Challenge Rubric" for each team member.

Conference: Teacher/student conferences are held to discuss the completed evaluations.

# Our Skin: Student Challenge

**STEM Lab Challenge:** Design a 3-dimensional model of the human skin. The model should contain the major structures of the skin. Each structure should be labeled and include a brief description of its function.

## You Should Know
Skin is your largest body organ. It does several jobs, which include physically protecting your bones, muscles, and internal organs; protecting your body from outside diseases; allowing you to feel and react to heat and cold; and using blood to regulate your body heat.

## Vocabulary Review
- dermis
- epidermis
- hypodermis
- pores
- sweat gland
- ectodermal tissue
- follicle
- oil gland
- subcutis

## Materials You May Need
- design materials: to be determined by student research

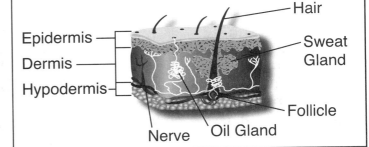

## Challenge Requirements
1. Research: Write a one- to two-page paper summarizing your research on the integumentary system and human skin. Cite your sources. Your paper may include two pictures.
2. Model: Label a drawing of your human skin model and explain your strategy.
3. Results: Record, analyze, and interpret test results.
4. Conclusion: Summarize the lab and what actually happened. It should include the purpose, a brief description of the test procedure, and explanation of results.
5. Reflection: Think about your team's choices for the skin model. Then complete the "Reflection" handout.
6. Evaluation: Think about your behavior and performance as a team member. Then complete the "Self-Evaluation Rubric."

## Steps to Follow
*Work with a team to complete the steps listed below. A team will have 3 or 4 members.*

Step 1:  Research the integumentary system and human skin.
Step 2:  Brainstorm ideas about how to design a human skin model to meet the requirements of the lab.
Step 3:  Draw a diagram of your design.
Step 4:  Construct the model.
Step 5:  Test the accuracy of the model by using your science book or other resources. Record the results of your comparisons.
Step 6:  Evaluate how well the items chosen for your model actually represent the parts of human skin.
Step 7:  Identify how to improve your design.
Step 8:  Make the needed changes.
Step 9:  Retest and reevaluate the improved design.
Step 10: Share the results.

# What Makes You Sick?: Teacher Information

## STEM Lab Overview

Students are challenged to design a 3-dimensional model of a virus. The model should include the two main parts of a virus: the nucleic acid core and capsid.

## Concepts

- Infectious diseases
- Viruses

## Standards for Grades 6–8

| NGSS | NCTM | ITEA | CCSS |
|---|---|---|---|
| -Growth, Development, and Reproduction of Organisms | -Problem Solving<br>-Communication<br>-Connections<br>-Representation | -Nature of Technology<br>-Technology and Society<br>-Technological World | -English Language Arts Standards:<br>   Science & Technical Subjects |

## Teaching Strategies

Step #1: Engage—Review concepts. Introduce the STEM lab. Discuss the challenge presented in the lab, providing students with an opportunity to connect previous knowledge to the problem they are to solve.

Step #2: Investigate—Students conduct research to gain an understanding of the major science concepts related to the topic, review possible solutions to the lab challenge, and formulate new ideas for solving the problem.

Step #3: Explore—Students apply research to design and test a model, process, or system to solve the problem presented in the challenge.

Step #4: Communicate—Students share results.

Step #5: Evaluate—Students are given an opportunity to reflect on what they have learned.

## Managing the Lab

- Set a deadline for project submission and presentations.
- Group students into collaborative teams and assign roles.
- Review prerequisite skills students need for doing the lab, such as measuring, weighing, constructing, recording data, graphing, and so on.
- Review science safety rules.
- Review lab cleanup procedures.
- Have the needed materials available, organized, and set up for easy access.
- Monitor teams and provide productive feedback.
- Leave enough time at the end of class for cleanup and debriefing.
- Designate area for project storage.

## Evaluation

Student Reflection: Students think about their team's choices for the design of the prototype. Students individually complete the "Reflection" handout.

Student Self-Evaluation: Students think about their behavior and performance as a team member. Students individually complete the "Self-Evaluation Rubric."

Lab Evaluation: The teacher completes the "Lab Challenge Rubric" for each team member.

Conference: Teacher/student conferences are held to discuss the completed evaluations.

# What Makes You Sick?: Student Challenge

**STEM Lab Challenge:** Design a 3-dimensional model of a virus. The model should include the two main parts of a virus: the nucleic acid core and capsid.

## You Should Know

Viruses cause many diseases such as the common cold, flu, measles, Ebola, and AIDS. A virus is not a cell. However, viruses can replicate, or make copies of themselves, once inside a living cell.

## Vocabulary Review

- disease
- host cell
- infectious
- pathogen
- replicate
- virus

## Materials You May Need

- design materials: to be determined by student research

## Challenge Requirements

1. Research: Write a one- to two-page paper summarizing your research on infectious diseases and viruses. Cite your sources. Your paper may include two pictures.
2. Model: Label a drawing of your virus model and explain your strategy.
3. Results: Record, analyze, and interpret test results.
4. Conclusion: Summarize the lab and what actually happened. It should include the purpose, a brief description of the test procedure, and explanation of results.
5. Reflection: Think about your team's choices for the virus model. Then complete the "Reflection" handout.
6. Evaluation: Think about your behavior and performance as a team member. Then complete the "Self-Evaluation Rubric."

## Steps to Follow

*Work with a team to complete the steps listed below. A team will have 3 or 4 members.*

Step 1: Research infectious diseases and viruses.
Step 2: Brainstorm ideas about how to design a virus model to meet the requirements of the lab.
Step 3: Draw a diagram of your design.
Step 4: Construct the model.
Step 5: Test the accuracy of the model by using your science book or other resources. Record the results of your comparisons.
Step 6: Evaluate how well the items chosen for your model actually represent the parts of the virus.
Step 7: Identify how to improve your design.
Step 8: Make the needed changes.
Step 9: Retest and reevaluate the improved design.
Step 10: Share the results.

# Meiosis: Teacher Information

## STEM Lab Overview

Students are challenged to design a model of meiosis that illustrates the phases in the process of producing human sex cells. Each phase should be labeled and include a brief explanation.

## Concepts

- Meiosis
- Sexual reproduction

## Standards for Grades 6–8

| NGSS | NCTM | ITEA | CCSS |
|---|---|---|---|
| -Growth, Development, and Reproduction of Organisms | -Problem Solving<br>-Communication<br>-Connections<br>-Representation | -Nature of Technology<br>-Technology and Society<br>-Technological World | -English Language Arts Standards:<br>   Science & Technical Subjects |

## Teaching Strategies

Step #1:  Engage—Review concepts. Introduce the STEM lab. Discuss the challenge presented in the lab, providing students with an opportunity to connect previous knowledge to the problem they are to solve.

Step #2:  Investigate—Students conduct research to gain an understanding of the major science concepts related to the topic, review possible solutions to the lab challenge, and formulate new ideas for solving the problem.

Step #3:  Explore—Students apply research to design and test a model, process, or system to solve the problem presented in the challenge.

Step #4:  Communicate—Students share results.

Step #5:  Evaluate—Students are given an opportunity to reflect on what they have learned.

## Managing the Lab

- Set a deadline for project submission and presentations.
- Group students into collaborative teams and assign roles.
- Review prerequisite skills students need for doing the lab, such as measuring, weighing, constructing, recording data, graphing, and so on.
- Review science safety rules.
- Review lab cleanup procedures.
- Have the needed materials available, organized, and set up for easy access.
- Monitor teams and provide productive feedback.
- Leave enough time at the end of class for cleanup and debriefing.
- Designate area for project storage.

## Evaluation

Student Reflection: Students think about their team's choices for the design of the prototype. Students individually complete the "Reflection" handout.

Student Self-Evaluation: Students think about their behavior and performance as a team member. Students individually complete the "Self-Evaluation Rubric."

Lab Evaluation: The teacher completes the "Lab Challenge Rubric" for each team member.

Conference: Teacher/student conferences are held to discuss the completed evaluations.

Reproduction/Heredity

# Meiosis: Student Challenge

**STEM Lab Challenge:** Design a model of meiosis that illustrates the phases in the process of producing a human sex cell. Each phase should be labeled and include a brief explanation.

## You Should Know

A human body produces two types of cells, body cells and sex cells. The process called **meiosis** produces sex cells.

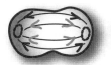

## Vocabulary Review
- chromosomes
- diploid cells
- meiosis
- nucleus
- sex cell
- sexual reproduction

## Materials You May Need
- various colors of yarn and pipe cleaners
- paper plates
- glue
- scissors
- other design materials: to be determined by student research

## Challenge Requirements

1. Research: Write a one- to two-page paper summarizing your research on sexual reproduction and the process of meiosis. Cite your sources. Your paper may include two pictures.
2. Model: Label a drawing of your meiosis model and explain your strategy.
3. Results: Record, analyze, and interpret test results.
4. Conclusion: Summarize the lab and what actually happened. It should include the purpose, a brief description of the test procedure, and explanation of results.
5. Reflection: Think about your team's choices for the meiosis model. Then complete the "Reflection" handout.
6. Evaluation: Think about your behavior and performance as a team member. Then complete the "Self-Evaluation Rubric."

## Steps to Follow

*Work with a team to complete the steps listed below. A team will have 3 or 4 members.*

Step 1: Research sexual reproduction and the process of meiosis.
Step 2: Brainstorm ideas about how to design a model of the process of meiosis to meet the requirements of the lab.
Step 3: Draw a diagram of your design.
Step 4: Construct the model.
Step 5: Test the accuracy of the model by using your science book or other resources. Record the results of your comparisons.
Step 6: Evaluate how well the items chosen for your model actually represent the five phases in the meiosis process.
Step 7: Identify how to improve your design.
Step 8: Make the needed changes.
Step 9: Retest and reevaluate the improved design.
Step 10: Share the results.

# DNA Extraction: Teacher Information

| STEM Lab Overview |
| --- |
| Students are challenged to design a process for extracting DNA from a fruit. |

| Concepts |
| --- |
| • DNA　　　• Genetic blueprint |

| Standards for Grades 6–8 | | | |
| --- | --- | --- | --- |
| **NGSS** | **NCTM** | **ITEA** | **CCSS** |
| -Growth, Development, and Reproduction of Organisms | -Problem Solving<br>-Communication<br>-Connections<br>-Representation | -Nature of Technology<br>-Technology and Society<br>-Technological World | -English Language Arts Standards:<br>　Science & Technical Subjects |

## Teaching Strategies

Step #1:　Engage—Review concepts. Introduce the STEM lab. Discuss the challenge presented in the lab, providing students with an opportunity to connect previous knowledge to the problem they are to solve.

Step #2:　Investigate—Students conduct research to gain an understanding of the major science concepts related to the topic, review possible solutions to the lab challenge, and formulate new ideas for solving the problem.

Step #3:　Explore—Students apply research to design and test a model, process, or system to solve the problem presented in the challenge.

Step #4:　Communicate—Students share results.

Step #5:　Evaluate—Students are given an opportunity to reflect on what they have learned.

## Managing the Lab

• Set a deadline for project submission and presentations.
• Group students into collaborative teams and assign roles.
• Review prerequisite skills students need for doing the lab, such as measuring, weighing, constructing, recording data, graphing, and so on.
• Review science safety rules.
• Review lab cleanup procedures.
• Have the needed materials available, organized, and set up for easy access.
• Monitor teams and provide productive feedback.
• Leave enough time at the end of class for cleanup and debriefing.
• Designate area for project storage.

## Evaluation

Student Reflection: Students think about their team's choices for the design of the prototype. Students individually complete the "Reflection" handout.

Student Self-Evaluation: Students think about their behavior and performance as a team member. Students individually complete the "Self-Evaluation Rubric."

Lab Evaluation: The teacher completes the "Lab Challenge Rubric" for each team member.

Conference: Teacher/student conferences are held to discuss the completed evaluations.

Reproduction/Heredity

# DNA Extraction: Student Challenge

**STEM Lab Challenge:** Design a process for extracting DNA from a fruit.

## You Should Know
All living organisms contain DNA, also known as deoxyribonucleic acid. DNA is a long molecule found in the nucleus of a cell. The DNA contains the genetic blueprint (code) for how an organism looks and functions.

## Vocabulary Review
- cell
- chromosomes
- DNA
- nucleic acid
- nucleus
- solution

## Materials You May Need
- a variety of fresh fruit (strawberries, bananas, and kiwi)
- water
- rubbing alcohol (70% or higher), ice cold
- table salt
- plastic bag
- coffee filter
- toothpick
- test tubes
- design materials: to be determined by student research

## Challenge Requirements
1. <u>Research</u>: Write a one- to two-page paper summarizing your research on DNA. Cite your sources. Your paper may include two pictures.
2. <u>Model</u>: Label a drawing of your process for extracting DNA from a fruit and explain your strategy.
3. <u>Results</u>: Record, analyze, and interpret test results.
4. <u>Conclusion</u>: Summarize the lab and what actually happened. It should include the purpose, a brief description of the test procedure, and explanation of results.
5. <u>Reflection</u>: Think about your team's choices for the DNA extraction process. Then complete the "Reflection" handout.
6. <u>Evaluation</u>: Think about your behavior and performance as a team member. Then complete the "Self-Evaluation Rubric."

## Steps to Follow
*Work with a team to complete the steps listed below. A team will have 3 or 4 members.*

Step 1: Research DNA.
Step 2: Choose a fruit. Brainstorm ideas about how to design a process for extracting DNA from it to meet the requirements of the lab.
Step 3: Draw a diagram of your process.
Step 4: Set up the process.
Step 5: Test the process. Record the results.
Step 6: Evaluate the performance of your process for DNA extraction.
Step 7: Identify how to improve your process.
Step 8: Make the needed changes.
Step 9: Retest and reevaluate the process.
Step 10: Share the results.

# Edible DNA: Teacher Information

## STEM Lab Overview

Students are challenged to design a 3-dimensional DNA model that illustrates the basic DNA structure and the rules of base pairing.

## Concepts

- DNA          • Double helix

## Standards for Grades 6–8

| NGSS | NCTM | ITEA | CCSS |
|---|---|---|---|
| -Growth, Development, and Reproduction of Organisms | -Problem Solving<br>-Communication<br>-Connections<br>-Representation | -Nature of Technology<br>-Technology and Society<br>-Technological World | -English Language Arts Standards:<br>    Science & Technical Subjects |

## Teaching Strategies

Step #1:   Engage—Review concepts. Introduce the STEM lab. Discuss the challenge presented in the lab, providing students with an opportunity to connect previous knowledge to the problem they are to solve.

Step #2:   Investigate—Students conduct research to gain an understanding of the major science concepts related to the topic, review possible solutions to the lab challenge, and formulate new ideas for solving the problem.

Step #3:   Explore—Students apply research to design and test a model, process, or system to solve the problem presented in the challenge.

Step #4:   Communicate—Students share results.

Step #5:   Evaluate—Students are given an opportunity to reflect on what they have learned.

## Managing the Lab

- Set a deadline for project submission and presentations.
- Group students into collaborative teams and assign roles.
- Review prerequisite skills students need for doing the lab, such as measuring, weighing, constructing, recording data, graphing, and so on.
- Review science safety rules.
- Review lab cleanup procedures.
- Have the needed materials available, organized, and set up for easy access.
- Monitor teams and provide productive feedback.
- Leave enough time at the end of class for cleanup and debriefing.
- Designate area for project storage.

## Evaluation

Student Reflection: Students think about their team's choices for the design of the prototype. Students individually complete the "Reflection" handout.

Student Self-Evaluation: Students think about their behavior and performance as a team member. Students individually complete the "Self-Evaluation Rubric."

Lab Evaluation: The teacher completes the "Lab Challenge Rubric" for each team member.

Conference: Teacher/student conferences are held to discuss the completed evaluations.

Reproduction/Heredity

# Edible DNA: Student Challenge

**STEM Lab Challenge:** Design a 3-dimensional DNA model that illustrates the basic DNA structure and the rules of base pairing.

## You Should Know

A single DNA molecule, or ladder, can have thousands of rungs or steps. The number of steps and how they are arranged form a genetic code. The genetic code determines the different kinds of inherited traits.

## Vocabulary Review

- chromosome
- DNA
- double helix
- gene
- trait

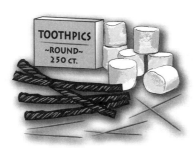

## Materials You May Need

- licorice
- colored marshmallows
- toothpicks
- other design materials: to be determined by student research

## Challenge Requirements

1. <u>Research</u>: Write a one- to two-page paper summarizing your research on DNA structure. Cite your sources. Your paper may include two pictures.
2. <u>Model</u>: Label a drawing of your DNA model and explain your strategy.
3. <u>Results</u>: Record, analyze, and interpret test results.
4. <u>Conclusion</u>: Summarize the lab and what actually happened. It should include the purpose, a brief description of the test procedure, and explanation of results.
5. <u>Reflection</u>: Think about your team's choices for the DNA model. Then complete the "Reflection" handout.
6. <u>Evaluation</u>: Think about your behavior and performance as a team member. Then complete the "Self-Evaluation Rubric."

## Steps to Follow

*Work with a team to complete the steps listed below. A team will have 3 or 4 members.*

Step 1: Research DNA structure.
Step 2: Brainstorm ideas about how you might make a DNA model to meet the requirements of the lab.
Step 3: Draw a diagram of your model.
Step 4: Construct your DNA model.
Step 5: Test the accuracy of your model using your science book or other resources. Record the results of your comparison.
Step 6: Evaluate how well the items chosen for your model actually represent the structure and base pairing of DNA.
Step 7: Identify how to improve the design of your model.
Step 8: Make the needed changes.
Step 9: Retest and reevaluate the improved design.
Step 10: Share your results.

# Chromosome Model: Teacher Information

## STEM Lab Overview

Students are challenged to design a 3-dimensional model of a chromosome with the chromatids and centromere labeled.

## Concepts

- Cell division
- Chromosomes

## Standards for Grades 6–8

| NGSS | NCTM | ITEA | CCSS |
|---|---|---|---|
| -Growth, Development, and Reproduction of Organisms | -Problem Solving<br>-Communication<br>-Connections<br>-Representation | -Nature of Technology<br>-Technology and Society<br>-Technological World | -English Language Arts Standards:<br>  Science & Technical Subjects |

## Teaching Strategies

Step #1:  Engage—Review concepts. Introduce the STEM lab. Discuss the challenge presented in the lab, providing students with an opportunity to connect previous knowledge to the problem they are to solve.

Step #2:  Investigate—Students conduct research to gain an understanding of the major science concepts related to the topic, review possible solutions to the lab challenge, and formulate new ideas for solving the problem.

Step #3:  Explore—Students apply research to design and test a model, process, or system to solve the problem presented in the challenge.

Step #4:  Communicate—Students share results.

Step #5:  Evaluate—Students are given an opportunity to reflect on what they have learned.

## Managing the Lab

- Set a deadline for project submission and presentations.
- Group students into collaborative teams and assign roles.
- Review prerequisite skills students need for doing the lab, such as measuring, weighing, constructing, recording data, graphing, and so on.
- Review science safety rules.
- Review lab cleanup procedures.
- Have the needed materials available, organized, and set up for easy access.
- Monitor teams and provide productive feedback.
- Leave enough time at the end of class for cleanup and debriefing.
- Designate area for project storage.

## Evaluation

Student Reflection: Students think about their team's choices for the design of the prototype. Students individually complete the "Reflection" handout.

Student Self-Evaluation: Students think about their behavior and performance as a team member. Students individually complete the "Self-Evaluation Rubric."

Lab Evaluation: The teacher completes the "Lab Challenge Rubric" for each team member.

Conference: Teacher/student conferences are held to discuss the completed evaluations.

Reproduction/Heredity

# Chromosome Model: Student Challenge

**STEM Lab Challenge:** Design a 3-dimensional model of a chromosome with the chromatids and centromere labeled.

## You Should Know
Chromosomes are rod-shaped strands of genetic material located inside the nucleus of plant and animal cells.

## Vocabulary Review
- cell division
- centromere
- chromatids
- chromosome
- nucleus

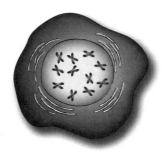

## Materials You May Need
- various colored pipe cleaners
- assortment of colored beads
- variety of colored markers
- paper, scissors, and glue
- other design materials: to be determined by student research

## Challenge Requirements
1. <u>Research</u>: Write a one- to two-page paper summarizing your research on cell division and chromosomes. Cite your sources. Your paper may include two pictures.
2. <u>Model</u>: Label a drawing of your chromosome model and explain your strategy.
3. <u>Results</u>: Record, analyze, and interpret test results.
4. <u>Conclusion</u>: Summarize the lab and what actually happened. It should include the purpose, a brief description of the test procedure, and explanation of results.
5. <u>Reflection</u>: Think about your team's choices for the chromosome model. Then complete the "Reflection" handout.
6. <u>Evaluation</u>: Think about your behavior and performance as a team member. Then complete the "Self-Evaluation Rubric."

## Steps to Follow
*Work with a team to complete the steps listed below. A team will have 3 or 4 members.*

Step 1:  Research cell division and chromosomes.
Step 2:  Brainstorm ideas about how to design a chromosome model to meet the requirements of the lab.
Step 3:  Draw a diagram of your design.
Step 4:  Construct the model.
Step 5:  Test the accuracy of the model by using your science book or other resources. Record the results of your comparisons.
Step 6:  Evaluate how well the items chosen for your model actually represent the parts of the chromosome.
Step 7:  Identify how to improve your design.
Step 8:  Make the needed changes.
Step 9:  Retest and reevaluate the improved design.
Step 10: Share the results.

# The Anatomy of a Flower: Teacher Information

## STEM Lab Overview

Students are challenged to design a 3-dimensional model of the anatomy of a flower. The important parts of the flower should be labeled and include a brief description.

## Concepts

- Anatomy of a flower     • Fertilization     • Pollination

## Standards for Grades 6–8

| NGSS | NCTM | ITEA | CCSS |
|---|---|---|---|
| -Growth, Development, and Reproduction of Organisms | -Problem Solving<br>-Communication<br>-Connections<br>-Representation | -Nature of Technology<br>-Technology and Society<br>-Technological World | -English Language Arts Standards:<br>Science & Technical Subjects |

## Teaching Strategies

Step #1:   Engage—Review concepts. Introduce the STEM lab. Discuss the challenge presented in the lab, providing students with an opportunity to connect previous knowledge to the problem they are to solve.

Step #2:   Investigate—Students conduct research to gain an understanding of the major science concepts related to the topic, review possible solutions to the lab challenge, and formulate new ideas for solving the problem.

Step #3:   Explore—Students apply research to design and test a model, process, or system to solve the problem presented in the challenge.

Step #4:   Communicate—Students share results.

Step #5:   Evaluate—Students are given an opportunity to reflect on what they have learned.

## Managing the Lab

- Set a deadline for project submission and presentations.
- Group students into collaborative teams and assign roles.
- Review prerequisite skills students need for doing the lab, such as measuring, weighing, constructing, recording data, graphing, and so on.
- Review science safety rules.
- Review lab cleanup procedures.
- Have the needed materials available, organized, and set up for easy access.
- Monitor teams and provide productive feedback.
- Leave enough time at the end of class for cleanup and debriefing.
- Designate area for project storage.

## Evaluation

Student Reflection: Students think about their team's choices for the design of the prototype. Students individually complete the "Reflection" handout.

Student Self-Evaluation: Students think about their behavior and performance as a team member. Students individually complete the "Self-Evaluation Rubric."

Lab Evaluation: The teacher completes the "Lab Challenge Rubric" for each team member.

Conference: Teacher/student conferences are held to discuss the completed evaluations.

Reproduction/Heredity

# The Anatomy of a Flower: Student Challenge

**STEM Lab Challenge:** Design a 3-dimensional model of the anatomy of a flower. The important parts of the flower should be labeled and include a brief description.

## You Should Know

Flowers perform the function of reproduction for some plants. Fertilization occurs when pollen from one plant is spread to another by insects and the wind.

## Vocabulary Review

- anther
- ovary
- petal
- sepal
- stigma
- filament
- ovule
- pistil
- stamen
- style

## Materials You May Need

- design materials: to be determined by student research

## Challenge Requirements

1. <u>Research</u>: Write a one- to two-page paper summarizing your research on flowering plants and pollination. Cite your sources. Your paper may include two pictures.
2. <u>Model</u>: Label a drawing of your flower model and explain your strategy.
3. <u>Results</u>: Record, analyze, and interpret test results.
4. <u>Conclusion</u>: Summarize the lab and what actually happened. It should include the purpose, a brief description of the test procedure, and explanation of results.
5. <u>Reflection</u>: Think about your team's choices for the flower model. Then complete the "Reflection" handout.
6. <u>Evaluation</u>: Think about your behavior and performance as a team member. Then complete the "Self-Evaluation Rubric."

## Steps to Follow

*Work with a team to complete the steps listed below. A team will have 3 or 4 members.*

Step 1: Research flowering plants and pollination.
Step 2: Brainstorm ideas about how you might make a flower model to meet the requirements of the lab.
Step 3: Draw a diagram of your model.
Step 4: Construct your flower model.
Step 5: Test the accuracy of your model by using your science book or other resources. Record the results of your comparison.
Step 6: Evaluate your flower model. Identify items selected to represent the various parts and assess how well the items chosen represent the actual parts of the flower.
Step 7: Identify how to improve the design of your model.
Step 8: Make the needed changes.
Step 9: Retest and reevaluate the improved design.
Step 10: Share your results.

# Cross-Pollination of Petunia Plants: Teacher Information

## STEM Lab Overview

Students are challenged to design a process for cross-pollination of two flowering petunia plants.

## Concepts

- Flower structure
- Pollination

## Standards for Grades 6–8

| NGSS | NCTM | ITEA | CCSS |
|---|---|---|---|
| -Growth, Development, and Reproduction of Organisms | -Problem Solving<br>-Communication<br>-Connections<br>-Representation | -Nature of Technology<br>-Technology and Society<br>-Technological World | -English Language Arts Standards:<br>    Science & Technical Subjects |

## Teaching Strategies

Step #1:   Engage—Review concepts. Introduce the STEM lab. Discuss the challenge presented in the lab, providing students with an opportunity to connect previous knowledge to the problem they are to solve.

Step #2:   Investigate—Students conduct research to gain an understanding of the major science concepts related to the topic, review possible solutions to the lab challenge, and formulate new ideas for solving the problem.

Step #3:   Explore—Students apply research to design and test a model, process, or system to solve the problem presented in the challenge.

Step #4:   Communicate—Students share results.

Step #5:   Evaluate—Students are given an opportunity to reflect on what they have learned.

## Managing the Lab

- Set a deadline for project submission and presentations.
- Group students into collaborative teams and assign roles.
- Review prerequisite skills students need for doing the lab, such as measuring, weighing, constructing, recording data, graphing, and so on.
- Review science safety rules.
- Review lab cleanup procedures.
- Have the needed materials available, organized, and set up for easy access.
- Monitor teams and provide productive feedback.
- Leave enough time at the end of class for cleanup and debriefing.
- Designate area for project storage.

## Evaluation

Student Reflection: Students think about their team's choices for the design of the prototype. Students individually complete the "Reflection" handout.

Student Self-Evaluation: Students think about their behavior and performance as a team member. Students individually complete the "Self-Evaluation Rubric."

Lab Evaluation: The teacher completes the "Lab Challenge Rubric" for each team member.

Conference: Teacher/student conferences are held to discuss the completed evaluations.

Reproduction/Heredity

# Cross-Pollination of Petunia Plants: Student Challenge

**STEM Lab Challenge:** Design a process for the cross-pollination of two flowering petunia plants.

## You Should Know

Pollination is the transfer of pollen from the stamens to the stigma of a flowering plant. The process of cross-pollinating occurs all the time in nature. Pollen is exchanged from one flower to another by insects and wind.

## Vocabulary Review

- cross-pollination
- fertilization
- pollination
- stamen
- stigma

## Materials You May Need

- one white and one dark-colored healthy, freshly bloomed petunia plant
- rubbing alcohol
- tweezers
- cotton ball
- other design materials: to be determined by student research

## Challenge Requirements

1. <u>Research</u>: Write a one- to two-page paper summarizing your research on the structure of a flower and the process of cross-pollination. Cite your sources. Your paper may include two pictures.
2. <u>Model</u>: Label a drawing of your cross-pollination process and explain your strategy.
3. <u>Results</u>: Record, analyze, and interpret test results.
4. <u>Conclusion</u>: Summarize the lab and what actually happened. It should include the purpose, a brief description of the test procedure, and explanation of results.
5. <u>Reflection</u>: Think about your team's choices for the cross-pollination process. Then complete the "Reflection" handout.
6. <u>Evaluation</u>: Think about your behavior and performance as a team member. Then complete the "Self-Evaluation Rubric."

## Steps to Follow

*Work with a team to complete the steps listed below. A team will have 3 or 4 members.*

Step 1: Research the structure of flowers and the process of cross-pollination.
Step 2: Brainstorm ideas about how you might design a process to cross-pollinate a flower to meet the requirements of the lab.
Step 3: Draw a diagram of your process.
Step 4: Set up the process.
Step 5: Test the process. Record the results.
Step 6: Evaluate the performance of your process.
Step 7: Identify how to improve the process.
Step 8: Make the needed changes.
Step 9: Retest and reevaluate the improved design.
Step 10: Share the results.

# Compost Chamber: Teacher Information

## STEM Lab Overview

Students are challenged to design a model of a compost chamber that will decompose organic waste.

## Concepts

- Nitrogen, oxygen, and carbon cycles
- Decomposition

## Standards for Grades 6–8

| NGSS | NCTM | ITEA | CCSS |
|---|---|---|---|
| -Matter and Energy in Organisms and Ecosystems | -Problem Solving<br>-Communication<br>-Connections<br>-Representation | -Nature of Technology<br>-Technology and Society<br>-Technological World | -English Language Arts Standards:<br>Science & Technical Subjects |

## Teaching Strategies

Step #1: Engage—Review concepts. Introduce the STEM lab. Discuss the challenge presented in the lab, providing students with an opportunity to connect previous knowledge to the problem they are to solve.

Step #2: Investigate—Students conduct research to gain an understanding of the major science concepts related to the topic, review possible solutions to the lab challenge, and formulate new ideas for solving the problem.

Step #3: Explore—Students apply research to design and test a model, process, or system to solve the problem presented in the challenge.

Step #4: Communicate—Students share results.

Step #5: Evaluate—Students are given an opportunity to reflect on what they have learned.

## Managing the Lab

- Set a deadline for project submission and presentations.
- Group students into collaborative teams and assign roles.
- Review prerequisite skills students need for doing the lab, such as measuring, weighing, constructing, recording data, graphing, and so on.
- Review science safety rules.
- Review lab cleanup procedures.
- Have the needed materials available, organized, and set up for easy access.
- Monitor teams and provide productive feedback.
- Leave enough time at the end of class for cleanup and debriefing.
- Designate area for project storage.

## Evaluation

Student Reflection: Students think about their team's choices for the design of the prototype. Students individually complete the "Reflection" handout.

Student Self-Evaluation: Students think about their behavior and performance as a team member. Students individually complete the "Self-Evaluation Rubric."

Lab Evaluation: The teacher completes the "Lab Challenge Rubric" for each team member.

Conference: Teacher/student conferences are held to discuss the completed evaluations.

# Compost Chamber: Student Challenge

**STEM Lab Challenge:** Design a model of a compost chamber that will decompose organic waste.

## You Should Know

Composting turns your organic waste into a valuable resource. By composting your yard and kitchen waste, you send less garbage to landfills. Your compost may then be used to grow a garden or potted plants.

## Vocabulary Review

- bacteria
- biodegradable
- carbon
- compost
- decompose
- humus
- microorganisms
- nitrogen
- organic matter

## Materials You May Need

- two-liter clear plastic bottle
- garden soil
- organic food waste
- grass clippings and dry leaves
- wide, clear tape
- sharp scissors or knife
- other design materials: to be determined by student research

## Challenge Requirements

1. Research: Write a one- to two-page paper summarizing your research on composting and decomposition. Cite your sources. Your paper may include two pictures.
2. Model: Label a drawing of your composting model and explain your strategy.
3. Results: Record, analyze, and interpret test results.
4. Conclusion: Summarize the lab and what actually happened. It should include the purpose, a brief description of the test procedure, and explanation of results.
5. Reflection: Think about your team's choices for the composting model. Then complete the "Reflection" handout.
6. Evaluation: Think about your behavior and performance as a team member. Then complete the "Self-Evaluation Rubric."

## Steps to Follow

*Work with a team to complete the steps listed below. A team will have 3 or 4 members.*

Step 1: Research composting and decomposition.
Step 2: Brainstorm ideas about how to design a compost model to meet the requirements of the lab. Think about the best way to layer organic materials.
Step 3: Draw a diagram of your design.
Step 4: Construct the model.
Step 5: Test the design.
Step 6: Evaluate how well the items chosen for your model actually decomposed.
Step 7: Identify how to improve your design.
Step 8: Make the needed changes.
Step 9: Retest and reevaluate the improved design.
Step 10: Share the results.

# A Human Shelter: Teacher Information

| STEM Lab Overview |
|---|
| Students are challenged to design a model of a human shelter inspired by an animal habitat. The shelter should provide protection against wind and rain. |

| Concepts |
|---|
| • Animal classification    • Biome |

| Standards for Grades 6–8 | | | |
|---|---|---|---|
| **NGSS** | **NCTM** | **ITEA** | **CCSS** |
| -Interdependent Relationships in Ecosystems | -Problem Solving<br>-Communication<br>-Connections<br>-Representation | -Nature of Technology<br>-Technology and Society<br>-Technological World | -English Language Arts Standards:<br>  Science & Technical Subjects |

### Teaching Strategies

Step #1:  Engage—Review concepts. Introduce the STEM lab. Discuss the challenge presented in the lab, providing students with an opportunity to connect previous knowledge to the problem they are to solve.

Step #2:  Investigate—Students conduct research to gain an understanding of the major science concepts related to the topic, review possible solutions to the lab challenge, and formulate new ideas for solving the problem.

Step #3:  Explore—Students apply research to design and test a model, process, or system to solve the problem presented in the challenge.

Step #4:  Communicate—Students share results.

Step #5:  Evaluate—Students are given an opportunity to reflect on what they have learned.

### Managing the Lab

- Set a deadline for project submission and presentations.
- Group students into collaborative teams and assign roles.
- Review prerequisite skills students need for doing the lab, such as measuring, weighing, constructing, recording data, graphing, and so on.
- Review science safety rules.
- Review lab cleanup procedures.
- Have the needed materials available, organized, and set up for easy access.
- Monitor teams and provide productive feedback.
- Leave enough time at the end of class for cleanup and debriefing.
- Designate area for project storage.

### Evaluation

Student Reflection: Students think about their team's choices for the design of the prototype. Students individually complete the "Reflection" handout.

Student Self-Evaluation: Students think about their behavior and performance as a team member. Students individually complete the "Self-Evaluation Rubric."

Lab Evaluation: The teacher completes the "Lab Challenge Rubric" for each team member.

Conference: Teacher/student conferences are held to discuss the completed evaluations.

**Ecosystems**

# A Human Shelter: Student Challenge

**STEM Lab Challenge:** Design a model of a human shelter inspired by an animal habitat. The shelter should provide protection against wind and rain.

## You Should Know
One of the essential requirements for animal and human survival is shelter. Throughout history, humans have made a variety of shelters based on the resources available to them.

## Vocabulary Review
- animal
- biome
- habitat
- shelter

## Materials You May Need
- design materials: to be determined by student research

## Challenge Requirements
1. Research: Write a one- to two-page paper summarizing your research on shelters used by animals and humans. Cite your sources. Your paper may include two pictures.
2. Model: Label a drawing of your human shelter model and explain your strategy.
3. Results: Record, analyze, and interpret test results.
4. Conclusion: Summarize the lab and what actually happened. It should include the purpose, a brief description of the test procedure, and explanation of results.
5. Reflection: Think about your team's choices for the human shelter model. Then complete the "Reflection" handout.
6. Evaluation: Think about your behavior and performance as a team member. Then complete the "Self-Evaluation Rubric."

## Steps to Follow
*Work with a team to complete the steps listed below. A team will have 3 or 4 members.*

Step 1: Research shelters used by animals and humans.
Step 2: Brainstorm ideas about how to design a human shelter to meet the requirements of the lab. Think about the type of materials you will use.
Step 3: Draw a diagram of your design.
Step 4: Construct the shelter.
Step 5: Test the design. Record the results.
Step 6: Evaluate the performance of your human shelter.
Step 7: Identify how to improve your design.
Step 8: Make the needed changes.
Step 9: Retest and reevaluate the improved design.
Step 10: Share the results.

# Hummingbird Feeder: Teacher Information

## STEM Lab Overview

Students are challenged to design a model of a feeder that will attract hummingbirds.

## Concepts

- Hummingbirds

## Standards for Grades 6–8

| NGSS | NCTM | ITEA | CCSS |
|---|---|---|---|
| -Interdependent Relationships in Ecosystems | -Problem Solving<br>-Communication<br>-Connections<br>-Representation | -Nature of Technology<br>-Technology and Society<br>-Technological World | -English Language Arts Standards:<br>    Science & Technical Subjects |

## Teaching Strategies

Step #1:  Engage—Review concepts. Introduce the STEM lab. Discuss the challenge presented in the lab, providing students with an opportunity to connect previous knowledge to the problem they are to solve.

Step #2:  Investigate—Students conduct research to gain an understanding of the major science concepts related to the topic, review possible solutions to the lab challenge, and formulate new ideas for solving the problem.

Step #3:  Explore—Students apply research to design and test a model, process, or system to solve the problem presented in the challenge.

Step #4:  Communicate—Students share results.

Step #5:  Evaluate—Students are given an opportunity to reflect on what they have learned.

## Managing the Lab

- Set a deadline for project submission and presentations.
- Group students into collaborative teams and assign roles.
- Review prerequisite skills students need for doing the lab, such as measuring, weighing, constructing, recording data, graphing, and so on.
- Review science safety rules.
- Review lab cleanup procedures.
- Have the needed materials available, organized, and set up for easy access.
- Monitor teams and provide productive feedback.
- Leave enough time at the end of class for cleanup and debriefing.
- Designate area for project storage.

## Evaluation

Student Reflection: Students think about their team's choices for the design of the prototype. Students individually complete the "Reflection" handout.

Student Self-Evaluation: Students think about their behavior and performance as a team member. Students individually complete the "Self-Evaluation Rubric."

Lab Evaluation: The teacher completes the "Lab Challenge Rubric" for each team member.

Conference: Teacher/student conferences are held to discuss the completed evaluations.

Ecosystems

# Hummingbird Feeder: Student Challenge

**STEM Lab Challenge:** Design a model of a feeder that will attract hummingbirds.

## You Should Know

Hummingbirds consume more than their own weight in nectar each day, and to do so they must visit hundreds of flowers. They store just enough energy to survive overnight.

## Vocabulary Review

- adaptations
- habitats
- metabolism
- mutualism
- nectar
- pollination
- symbiosis

## Materials You May Need

- plastic bottle with lid
- small plastic container with flexible, tight-fitting lid
- strong rubber band
- sugar and water (food for hummingbirds)
- string
- pen
- paper hole punch
- awl or drill
- other design materials: to be determined by student research

## Challenge Requirements

1. Research: Write a one- to two-page paper summarizing your research on hummingbirds and their feeding relationship with flowers. Cite your sources. Your paper may include two pictures.
2. Model: Label a drawing of your hummingbird feeder and explain your strategy.
3. Results: Record, analyze, and interpret test results.
4. Conclusion: Summarize the lab and what actually happened. It should include the purpose, a brief description of the test procedure, and explanation of results.
5. Reflection: Think about your team's choices for the hummingbird feeder. Then complete the "Reflection" handout.
6. Evaluation: Think about your behavior and performance as a team member. Then complete the "Self-Evaluation Rubric."

## Steps to Follow

*Work with a team to complete the steps listed below. A team will have 3 or 4 members.*

Step 1: Research hummingbirds and their feeding relationship with flowers.
Step 2: Brainstorm ideas about how to design a hummingbird feeder to meet the requirements of the lab.
Step 3: Draw a diagram of your design.
Step 4: Construct the hummingbird feeder.
Step 5: Test your feeder. Record the results.
Step 6: Evaluate the performance of your hummingbird feeder.
Step 7: Identify how to improve your design.
Step 8: Make the needed changes.
Step 9: Retest and reevaluate the improved design.
Step 10: Share your results.

# Environmentally Friendly Soda Can Carrier: Teacher Information

## STEM Lab Overview

Students are challenged to design a model of a carrier for six aluminum soda cans that is environmentally friendly and animal safe. It should be sturdy and easy to carry.

## Concepts

- Wildlife conservation
- Alternatives for plastics

## Standards for Grades 6–8

| NGSS | NCTM | ITEA | CCSS |
|---|---|---|---|
| -Interdependent Relationships in Ecosystems | -Problem Solving<br>-Communication<br>-Connections<br>-Representation | -Nature of Technology<br>-Technology and Society<br>-Technological World | -English Language Arts Standards:<br>Science & Technical Subjects |

## Teaching Strategies

Step #1: Engage—Review concepts. Introduce the STEM lab. Discuss the challenge presented in the lab, providing students with an opportunity to connect previous knowledge to the problem they are to solve.

Step #2: Investigate—Students conduct research to gain an understanding of the major science concepts related to the topic, review possible solutions to the lab challenge, and formulate new ideas for solving the problem.

Step #3: Explore—Students apply research to design and test a model, process, or system to solve the problem presented in the challenge.

Step #4: Communicate—Students share results.

Step #5: Evaluate—Students are given an opportunity to reflect on what they have learned.

## Managing the Lab

- Set a deadline for project submission and presentations.
- Group students into collaborative teams and assign roles.
- Review prerequisite skills students need for doing the lab, such as measuring, weighing, constructing, recording data, graphing, and so on.
- Review science safety rules.
- Review lab cleanup procedures.
- Have the needed materials available, organized, and set up for easy access.
- Monitor teams and provide productive feedback.
- Leave enough time at the end of class for cleanup and debriefing.
- Designate area for project storage.

## Evaluation

Student Reflection: Students think about their team's choices for the design of the prototype. Students individually complete the "Reflection" handout.

Student Self-Evaluation: Students think about their behavior and performance as a team member. Students individually complete the "Self-Evaluation Rubric."

Lab Evaluation: The teacher completes the "Lab Challenge Rubric" for each team member.

Conference: Teacher/student conferences are held to discuss the completed evaluations.

Ecosystems

# Environmentally Friendly Soda Can Carrier: Student Challenge

**STEM Lab Challenge:** Design a model of a carrier for six aluminum soda cans that is environmentally friendly and animal safe. It should be sturdy and easy to carry.

## You Should Know
Plastic ring-type holders found on six-packs of aluminum soda cans can sometimes end up in the water and other environments, ensnaring and endangering the wildlife living there. Engineers work on ways to improve packaging systems to reduce litter and protect animals.

## Vocabulary Review
- biodegradable
- environment
- litter
- natural resource
- non-biodegradable
- photo-degradation
- pollution
- recyclable
- reusable

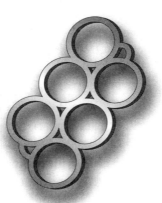

## Materials You May Need
- six full, unopened aluminum soda cans
- other design materials: to be determined by student research

## Challenge Requirements
1. <u>Research</u>: Write a one- to two-page paper summarizing your research on alternatives for plastic soda can carriers. Cite your sources. Your paper may include two pictures.
2. <u>Model</u>: Label a drawing of your soda can carrier model and explain your strategy.
3. <u>Results</u>: Record, analyze, and interpret test results.
4. <u>Conclusion</u>: Summarize the lab and what actually happened. It should include the purpose, a brief description of the test procedure, and explanation of results.
5. <u>Reflection</u>: Think about your team's choices for the soda can carrier model. Then complete the "Reflection" handout.
6. <u>Evaluation</u>: Think about your behavior and performance as a team member. Then complete the "Self-Evaluation Rubric."

## Steps to Follow
*Work with a team to complete the steps listed below. A team will have 3 or 4 members.*

Step 1: Research alternatives for plastic soda can carriers.

Step 2: Brainstorm ideas about how to design a soda can carrier to meet the requirements of the lab. Think about the strength and durability of the materials you use.

Step 3: Draw a diagram of your design.

Step 4: Construct the soda can carrier.

Step 5: Test the design. Record the results.

Step 6: Evaluate the performance of your soda can carrier.

Step 7: Identify how to improve your design.

Step 8: Make the needed changes.

Step 9: Retest and reevaluate the improved design.

Step 10: Share the results.

# Ant Village: Teacher Information

## STEM Lab Overview

Students are challenged to design a model of a habitat that can be used to view and document ant behavior.

## Concepts

- Invertebrates
- Arthropods
- Community
- Metamorphosis

## Standards for Grades 6–8

| NGSS | NCTM | ITEA | CCSS |
|---|---|---|---|
| -Interdependent Relationships in Ecosystems | -Problem Solving<br>-Communication<br>-Connections<br>-Representation | -Nature of Technology<br>-Technology and Society<br>-Technological World | -English Language Arts Standards:<br>   Science & Technical Subjects |

## Teaching Strategies

Step #1:  Engage—Review concepts. Introduce the STEM lab. Discuss the challenge presented in the lab, providing students with an opportunity to connect previous knowledge to the problem they are to solve.

Step #2:  Investigate—Students conduct research to gain an understanding of the major science concepts related to the topic, review possible solutions to the lab challenge, and formulate new ideas for solving the problem.

Step #3:  Explore—Students apply research to design and test a model, process, or system to solve the problem presented in the challenge.

Step #4:  Communicate—Students share results.

Step #5:  Evaluate—Students are given an opportunity to reflect on what they have learned.

## Managing the Lab

- Set a deadline for project submission and presentations.
- Group students into collaborative teams and assign roles.
- Review prerequisite skills students need for doing the lab, such as measuring, weighing, constructing, recording data, graphing, and so on.
- Review science safety rules.
- Review lab cleanup procedures.
- Have the needed materials available, organized, and set up for easy access.
- Monitor teams and provide productive feedback.
- Leave enough time at the end of class for cleanup and debriefing.
- Designate area for project storage.

## Evaluation

Student Reflection: Students think about their team's choices for the design of the prototype. Students individually complete the "Reflection" handout.

Student Self-Evaluation: Students think about their behavior and performance as a team member. Students individually complete the "Self-Evaluation Rubric."

Lab Evaluation: The teacher completes the "Lab Challenge Rubric" for each team member.

Conference: Teacher/student conferences are held to discuss the completed evaluations.

# Ant Village: Student Challenge

**STEM Lab Challenge:** Design a model of a habitat that can be used to view and document ant behavior.

## You Should Know

Ant colonies need sheltered places to nest and take care of their offspring. They have a system that divides the labor. Amazingly, they communicate with each other and are able to solve complex problems.

## Vocabulary Review

- antennae
- colony
- drones
- exoskeleton
- external stimuli
- insect
- nest
- pheromones
- queen
- soldier
- worker ants

## Materials You May Need

- aquarium or large glass jar with lid
- ants
- dark paper
- tape
- sand
- sugar water
- sponge
- other design materials: to be determined by student research

## Challenge Requirements

1. <u>Research</u>: Write a one- to two-page paper summarizing your research on ant communities. Cite your sources. Your paper may include two pictures.
2. <u>Model</u>: Label a drawing of your ant village and explain your strategy.
3. <u>Results</u>: Record, analyze, and interpret test results.
4. <u>Conclusion</u>: Summarize the lab and what actually happened. It should include the purpose, a brief description of the test procedure, and explanation of results.
5. <u>Reflection</u>: Think about your team's choices for the ant village. Then complete the "Reflection" handout.
6. <u>Evaluation</u>: Think about your behavior and performance as a team member. Then complete the "Self-Evaluation Rubric."

## Steps to Follow

*Work with a team to complete the steps listed below. A team will have 3 or 4 members.*

Step 1: Research ant communities.
Step 2: Brainstorm ideas about how to design an ant village to meet the requirements of the lab. Think about how to document the ants' behavior.
Step 3: Draw a diagram of your design.
Step 4: Construct the ant village.
Step 5: Test the design. Record the results.
Step 6: Evaluate how well the items chosen for your ant village actually represent an ant community.
Step 7: Identify how to improve your design.
Step 8: Make the needed changes.
Step 9: Retest and reevaluate the improved design.
Step 10: Share the results.

# Freshwater Ecosystem: Teacher Information

## STEM Lab Overview

Students are challenged to design a model of a closed freshwater ecosystem. The model should contain a habitat that will sustain the life of two guppies and two pond snails for seven days.

## Concepts

- Freshwater ecosystems
- Nitrogen, oxygen, and carbon cycles

## Standards for Grades 6–8

| NGSS | NCTM | ITEA | CCSS |
|---|---|---|---|
| -Matter and Energy in Organisms and Ecosystems | -Problem Solving<br>-Communication<br>-Connections<br>-Representation | -Nature of Technology<br>-Technology and Society<br>-Technological World | -English Language Arts Standards:<br>    Science & Technical Subjects |

## Teaching Strategies

Step #1:   Engage—Review concepts. Introduce the STEM lab. Discuss the challenge presented in the lab, providing students with an opportunity to connect previous knowledge to the problem they are to solve.

Step #2:   Investigate—Students conduct research to gain an understanding of the major science concepts related to the topic, review possible solutions to the lab challenge, and formulate new ideas for solving the problem.

Step #3:   Explore—Students apply research to design and test a model, process, or system to solve the problem presented in the challenge.

Step #4:   Communicate—Students share results.

Step #5:   Evaluate—Students are given an opportunity to reflect on what they have learned.

## Managing the Lab

- Set a deadline for project submission and presentations.
- Group students into collaborative teams and assign roles.
- Review prerequisite skills students need for doing the lab, such as measuring, weighing, constructing, recording data, graphing, and so on.
- Review science safety rules.
- Review lab cleanup procedures.
- Have the needed materials available, organized, and set up for easy access.
- Monitor teams and provide productive feedback.
- Leave enough time at the end of class for cleanup and debriefing.
- Designate area for project storage.

## Evaluation

Student Reflection: Students think about their team's choices for the design of the prototype. Students individually complete the "Reflection" handout.

Student Self-Evaluation: Students think about their behavior and performance as a team member. Students individually complete the "Self-Evaluation Rubric."

Lab Evaluation: The teacher completes the "Lab Challenge Rubric" for each team member.

Conference: Teacher/student conferences are held to discuss the completed evaluations.

# Freshwater Ecosystem: Student Challenge

**STEM Lab Challenge:** Design a model of a closed freshwater ecosystem. The model should contain a habitat that will sustain the life of two guppies and two pond snails for seven days.

## You Should Know
Ecosystems are a careful balance of their biotic and abiotic factors as well as the living organisms within them.

## Vocabulary Review
- abiotic
- biotic
- carbon cycle
- consumers
- decomposers
- food web
- freshwater ecosystem
- nitrogen cycle
- oxygen cycle
- producers

## Materials You May Need
- large jar with lid (1/2 gallon or 2 liter)
- two guppies
- two pond snails
- two aquatic plants
- aquarium pebbles
- 60-watt light bulb
- small dip net
- ruler
- other design materials: to be determined by student research

## Challenge Requirements
1. <u>Research</u>: Write a one- to two-page paper summarizing your research on abiotic and biotic factors in a freshwater ecosystem, guppies, and snails. Cite your sources. Your paper may include two pictures.
2. <u>Model</u>: Label a drawing of your freshwater ecosystem model and explain your strategy.
3. <u>Results</u>: Record, analyze, and interpret test results.
4. <u>Conclusion</u>: Summarize the lab and what actually happened. It should include the purpose, a brief description of the test procedure, and explanation of results.
5. <u>Reflection</u>: Think about your team's choices for the freshwater ecosystem model. Then complete the "Reflection" handout.
6. <u>Evaluation</u>: Think about your behavior and performance as a team member. Then complete the "Self-Evaluation Rubric."

## Steps to Follow
*Work with a team to complete the steps listed below. A team will have 3 or 4 members.*

Step 1:  Research abiotic and biotic factors in a freshwater ecosystem, guppies, and snails.

Step 2:  Brainstorm ideas about how to design an ecosystem model to meet the requirements of the lab.

Step 3:  Draw a diagram of your design.

Step 4:  Construct the model.

Step 5:  Test the design. Record the results.

Step 6:  Evaluate how well the items chosen for your model actually represent the parts of an ecosystem.

Step 7:  Identify how to improve your design.

Step 8:  Make the needed changes.

Step 9:  Retest and reevaluate the improved design.

Step 10: Share the results.

# Pollinator Ecosystem: Teacher Information

## STEM Lab Overview

Students are challenged to design a model of a pollinator ecosystem that will attract butterflies and moths.

## Concepts

- Ecosystems
- Insects
- Pollinator

## Standards for Grades 6–8

| NGSS | NCTM | ITEA | CCSS |
|---|---|---|---|
| -Interdependent Relationships in Ecosystems | -Problem Solving<br>-Communication<br>-Connections<br>-Representation | -Nature of Technology<br>-Technology and Society<br>-Technological World | -English Language Arts Standards:<br>   Science & Technical Subjects |

## Teaching Strategies

Step #1:   Engage—Review concepts. Introduce the STEM lab. Discuss the challenge presented in the lab, providing students with an opportunity to connect previous knowledge to the problem they are to solve.

Step #2:   Investigate—Students conduct research to gain an understanding of the major science concepts related to the topic, review possible solutions to the lab challenge, and formulate new ideas for solving the problem.

Step #3:   Explore—Students apply research to design and test a model, process, or system to solve the problem presented in the challenge.

Step #4:   Communicate—Students share results.

Step #5:   Evaluate—Students are given an opportunity to reflect on what they have learned.

## Managing the Lab

- Set a deadline for project submission and presentations.
- Group students into collaborative teams and assign roles.
- Review prerequisite skills students need for doing the lab, such as measuring, weighing, constructing, recording data, graphing, and so on.
- Review science safety rules.
- Review lab cleanup procedures.
- Have the needed materials available, organized, and set up for easy access.
- Monitor teams and provide productive feedback.
- Leave enough time at the end of class for cleanup and debriefing.
- Designate area for project storage.

## Evaluation

Student Reflection: Students think about their team's choices for the design of the prototype. Students individually complete the "Reflection" handout.

Student Self-Evaluation: Students think about their behavior and performance as a team member. Students individually complete the "Self-Evaluation Rubric."

Lab Evaluation: The teacher completes the "Lab Challenge Rubric" for each team member.

Conference: Teacher/student conferences are held to discuss the completed evaluations.

Ecosystems

# Pollinator Ecosystem: Student Challenge

**STEM Lab Challenge:** Design a model of a pollinator ecosystem that will attract butterflies and moths.

## You Should Know
Habitat loss is the main reason for the population decline of butterflies and moths. Butterflies and moths can disappear rapidly if the environment they rely on changes.

## Vocabulary Review
- adult
- caterpillar
- ecosystem
- habitat
- larvae
- moth
- pupa
- butterfly
- chrysalis
- egg
- insect
- metamorphosis
- pollinator
- pupate

## Materials You May Need
- gardening tools
- other design materials: to be determined by student research

## Challenge Requirements
1. <u>Research</u>: Write a one- to two-page paper summarizing your research on butterfly and moth habitats. Cite your sources. Your paper may include two pictures.
2. <u>Model</u>: Label a drawing of your ecosystem model and explain your strategy.
3. <u>Results</u>: Record, analyze, and interpret test results.
4. <u>Conclusion</u>: Summarize the lab and what actually happened. It should include the purpose, a brief description of the test procedure, and explanation of results.
5. <u>Reflection</u>: Think about your team's choices for the pollinator ecosystem model. Then complete the "Reflection" handout.
6. <u>Evaluation</u>: Think about your behavior and performance as a team member. Then complete the "Self-Evaluation Rubric."

## Steps to Follow
*Work with a team to complete the steps listed below. A team will have 3 or 4 members.*

Step 1: Research butterfly and moth habitats.
Step 2: Brainstorm ideas about how to design an ecosystem to meet the requirements of the lab. Think about the kind of plants and flowers you will need.
Step 3: Draw a diagram of your design.
Step 4: Construct your ecosystem.
Step 5: Test the design. Record the results.
Step 6: Evaluate how well the items chosen for your ecosystem actually attracted butterflies and moths.
Step 7: Identify how to improve your design.
Step 8: Make the needed changes.
Step 9: Retest and reevaluate the improved design.
Step 10: Share the results.

# Hydroponic Window Farm: Teacher Information

## STEM Lab Overview

Students are challenged to design a model of a vertical window farm that uses a hydroponic gardening system to grow herbs.

## Concepts

- Hydroponic gardening systems
- Photosynthesis
- Variables affecting plant growth

## Standards for Grades 6–8

| NGSS | NCTM | ITEA | CCSS |
|------|------|------|------|
| -Matter and Energy in Organisms and Ecosystems | -Problem Solving<br>-Communication<br>-Connections<br>-Representation | -Nature of Technology<br>-Technology and Society<br>-Technological World | -English Language Arts Standards:<br>  Science & Technical Subjects |

## Teaching Strategies

Step #1:  Engage—Review concepts. Introduce the STEM lab. Discuss the challenge presented in the lab, providing students with an opportunity to connect previous knowledge to the problem they are to solve.

Step #2:  Investigate—Students conduct research to gain an understanding of the major science concepts related to the topic, review possible solutions to the lab challenge, and formulate new ideas for solving the problem.

Step #3:  Explore—Students apply research to design and test a model, process, or system to solve the problem presented in the challenge.

Step #4:  Communicate—Students share results.

Step #5:  Evaluate—Students are given an opportunity to reflect on what they have learned.

## Managing the Lab

- Set a deadline for project submission and presentations.
- Group students into collaborative teams and assign roles.
- Review prerequisite skills students need for doing the lab, such as measuring, weighing, constructing, recording data, graphing, and so on.
- Review science safety rules.
- Review lab cleanup procedures.
- Have the needed materials available, organized, and set up for easy access.
- Monitor teams and provide productive feedback.
- Leave enough time at the end of class for cleanup and debriefing.
- Designate area for project storage.

## Evaluation

Student Reflection: Students think about their team's choices for the design of the prototype. Students individually complete the "Reflection" handout.

Student Self-Evaluation: Students think about their behavior and performance as a team member. Students individually complete the "Self-Evaluation Rubric."

Lab Evaluation: The teacher completes the "Lab Challenge Rubric" for each team member.

Conference: Teacher/student conferences are held to discuss the completed evaluations.

# Hydroponic Window Farm: Student Challenge

**STEM Lab Challenge:** Design a model of a vertical window farm that uses a hydroponic gardening system to grow herbs.

## You Should Know
A window farm system allows plants to grow in a window with moderate sunlight throughout the year.

## Vocabulary Review
- hydroponics
- nonvascular plants
- photosynthesis
- plant nutrients
- producers
- respiration
- vascular plants

## Materials You May Need
- herb seeds
- other design materials: to be determined by student research

## Challenge Requirements
1. <u>Research</u>: Write a one- to two-page paper summarizing your research on hydroponic gardening and vertical window farming technology. Cite your sources. Your paper may include two pictures.
2. <u>Model</u>: Label a drawing of your window farm system and explain your strategy.
3. <u>Results</u>: Record, analyze, and interpret test results.
4. <u>Conclusion</u>: Summarize the lab and what actually happened. It should include the purpose, a brief description of the test procedure, and explanation of results.
5. <u>Reflection</u>: Think about your team's choices for the window farm system. Then complete the "Reflection" handout.
6. <u>Evaluation</u>: Think about your behavior and performance as a team member. Then complete the "Self-Evaluation Rubric."

## Steps to Follow
*Work with a team to complete the steps listed below. A team will have 3 or 4 members.*

Step 1: Research hydroponic gardening and vertical window farming technology.
Step 2: Brainstorm ideas about how to design a window farm to meet the requirements of the lab. Think about the size and placement of your system.
Step 3: Draw a diagram of your design.
Step 4: Construct the model.
Step 5: Test the design. Record the results.
Step 6: Evaluate the performance of your window farm system.
Step 7: Identify how to improve your design.
Step 8: Make the needed changes.
Step 9: Retest and reevaluate the improved design.
Step 10: Share the results.